A Trade in Death

An Economics Mystery

CB

Scott Brunger

Emilie,

May you go far !

Scott

Friendship Press • New York

Editorial Offices:
475 Riverside Drive, New York, NY 10115

Distribution Offices:
P.O. Box 37844, Cincinnati, OH 45222-0844

Library of Congress Cataloging-in-Publication Data

Brunger, Scott
   A trade in death : an economics mystery / by Scott
Brunger.
      p. cm.
   ISBN 0-377-00265-8
      1. Economists—Africa—Fiction. 2. Murder—Africa—Fiction.
I. Title
PS3552.R7998M87   1993
813'.54—dc20   93-23202
                                                                        CIP

A Trade in Death

⁊

Contents

CB

Preface

CR

A TRADE IN DEATH is based on living and working in Africa during a period of twenty-five years. Back in 1968 the Frontier Internship in Mission Program sent my wife and me as volunteers for the World Student Christian Federation in Benin and Togo. At the end of our service in 1971, the Methodist Church of Benin and Togo invited us to return for two more years to start a conference center. The Christian Conference and Lay Training Center in Porto-Novo, Benin, has continued under African directors ever since. Upon returning to the United States in 1974, I studied economic development in graduate school while my wife finished seminary. My dissertation topic on the development of the internal market in Algeria, Ivory Coast, and Nigeria permitted me to do research on pre-colonial economies in North and West Africa. Following graduate school I accepted a position at Maryville College, a Presbyterian liberal arts college in Tennessee, and my wife became pastor of Highland Presbyterian Church. Since then I have made four trips to Africa to visit YMCA and church-sponsored grassroots development projects.

The hero of *A Trade in Death* is a composite of many dedicated Christian professionals whom I worked with in Africa.

Their witness in difficult circumstances is the shining light that keeps me hopeful for Africa's future.

Although Miseria is not a real country, every effort has been made to portray accurately life in Western and Central Africa. To this end the author is grateful for help from the Reverend and Mrs. Kimani Githieya, Dr. Elizabeth Perez-Reilly, James Gomez, Jr., and Rocio Huet-Cox, M.D. He also appreciates literary advice from Drs. Arthur Bushing and Roland Tapp.

The author wishes to thank his family for critical support and typing. Helping with questions and observations were his students in African studies and economic development courses.

List of Characters

ભ

Elijah Abobo: jailed con man

Assistant Minister Asaba: of the Ministry of Finance

Dr. Biggles: British linguist

Ahmad Boma: Miserian lawyer

Assistant Minister Bongo: of the Commission on Higher Education

Karla Curmudgeon: British economist

Inspector De Almeida: Immigration Director at the airport

Dr. Dossou: economist at the National University

Francis Falco: American economist and pilot

Francesca: hostess to Ben in village, wife of Salvador

Dean Gomez: Dean of the National University, Miserian historian

Francisco Gomez: brother of Dean Gomez

Felipe Hudunu: Miserian student, nephew of murder victim

Ilena Hudunu: daughter of murder victim

Xavier Hudunu: Miserian economist, murder victim

Lucia: secretary to Minister of Tourism

Rosa Lugner: caterer at the Grand Hotel

Benjamin Mchunguzi Maluum: Kenyan economist, Regional Secretary of the World Economics Association

Manga: treasurer of the Grand Hotel

Cristobal Mulama: liaison to Interpol, investigator of the Hudunu murder

Musa: director of the Grand Hotel

Philippe Petard: French economist

Paul Piccione: American economist and pilot

Dr. Rivera: Puerto Rican forestry expert

Salina: secretary to the Minister of the Interior

Salvador: host to Ben in village, husband of Francesca

Samuel: headwaiter at the Grand Hotel

Corporal Sodunu: investigator at the central police station

Dr. Stepan: East European economist

Teresa: friend of Señora Gomez and Ben

Traficant: French owner of import-export business

Victor Vodumanyon: Nigerian economist

Dr. Zande: Miserian economist

Chapter I

Big Ones and Little Ones

ᑲ

THE RISING SUN REVEALED A MAN lying languidly on a sand dune in front of the Grand Hotel. He wore an African shirt and swim trunks. His beach towel was wrapped over him. Sand flies moved away from him as the towel flapped in the ocean breeze. His head was turned away from the sun and from the hotel. Tourists on the beach did not see that he was dead.

On the night flight from London, Benjamin Mchunguzi Maluum, Ph.D., stretched his tired legs as the cabin crew prepared to serve breakfast. Light blazed in as the passenger in front of him lifted a shade to look out. Adjusting his eyes, Ben could see thick clouds ahead and green forest on the ground. The view indicated that the Air Miseria Boeing 707 had traversed the Sahara Desert.

His seat mates, a father and son from Miseria, returned from the toilet and squeezed around many packages into their seats. The father looked at him. "Dr. Chunguzi."

Ben realized that Miserians did not speak Swahili, as he did, or another Bantu language that used the prefix "Um" before the name "Mchunguzi." However, they shared the tra-

3

dition of stating the family name first before his given name "Maluum."

"Did you awaken well?" the father asked, translating into Spanish a traditional morning greeting.

"I awakened well, because I am home in Africa," replied Ben with a smile. "But I do not sleep well in flight any more."

"Perhaps Kenya Airways has better planes?" suggested the old man challenging him.

Although it did have better planes for its European flights, Ben preferred to be diplomatic. "When I was twenty years younger, like your son, I thought all planes were comfortable compared to the old buses in our town." They all smiled. "Now I cannot sleep comfortably on any of them. Did you both awaken well?"

"Yes, well. Thank God," the large sixty-year-old replied sincerely, unaware that his intermittent snores had interrupted Ben throughout the night.

The son waited his turn and then answered politely, "Yes, well." He looked "well" in his tailored European suit as he tightened his tie self-consciously.

The father asked, "Are you staying at the new American hotel?"

"I prefer African-owned hotels, so the management fees and profits stay to develop the local economy," answered Ben, eyeing the many packages they were bringing back.

"Oh, yes," the father half-heartedly agreed. "But we are bringing these back for our business, Santiago Import-Export. We had to go to Spain for the funeral of my son's adopted father, so now we are bringing back goods to pay for the trip."

"Who was your son's adopted father?"

"Old man Santiago. He needed to transfer majority ownership of his business to a Miserian twenty years ago before the government nationalized foreign-owned businesses. He adopted my baby, so the child would own the business while under his guardianship. That way he could control under family law what he could no longer own under commercial law."

Surprised, Ben asked, "So you gave him your son to help him?"

They both grinned shrewdly. The father went on. "No, I remained as Santiago's employee and took care of the boy. When he became twenty-one, my boy took over the business and Santiago retired. Now we have buried him in his homeland, and we have the business."

Ben looked hard. "Is it not your son's business?"

The father declared triumphantly, "We are Africans, are we not? My son's business is my business!"

"What kind of goods do you sell?" ventured Ben, knowing that continental businessmen were often reticent about their trade.

"We bring mostly electronic stereos, VCRs, and cameras. They are safer carried with us by air," the father replied candidly.

"How about typewriters and calculators for business?"

"We get them through the port."

"But they are electronic too. Why do they come by ship?"

"The customs is less for business products, and the Miserian port officials do not steal them like consumer products."

"I see. How much is customs duty on a VCR and video-camera?"

"One hundred percent duty, payable in foreign currency."

Ben worried. "I am organizing a conference of economists in Miseria and brought electronic equipment to videotape the speeches. Will I have to pay duty on it?"

"Yes. Is it new?"

"It is still under the one-year warranty."

"That doesn't matter. Is it a good brand?"

"Japanese."

"I will buy it from you. You can use it during the conference. Then I will sell it to someone else," the old man said eagerly.

Ben wavered. "I expect a representative from the National University will help clear the equipment through Customs. If necessary our World Economics Association will contribute it to them, so it will belong to a government institution."

"I will give you the price you paid for it."

"No. My employer bought it. I do not have the right to sell it to you."

"But you would give it to them?"

"Their university is a member of our association."

The arrival of breakfast ended the bargaining. Though it was generic airline food, Ben ate hungrily, not knowing if he would have the leisure to eat soon again after landing. The father attacked his meal with relish, using his fingers much of the time. His son demonstrated meticulous European manners. He cut each roll with his knife and spread jam and cheese on it before each bite. He was still eating long after the other two finished.

While he sipped his morning tea, Ben consulted his watch and discovered the scheduled time of arrival was still an hour away. To forestall further conversation, he consulted his list of things to do in Miseria:

1. "Call Xavier Hudunu." The man in charge of local arrangements should be at the airport. He had not been home for the past two weeks when Ben called.

2. "Receive the permit to convene the conference." Miseria's Minister of the Interior had promised it when they met three months ago. Under Napoleonic Law in effect in Miseria, the World Economics Association Regional Conference could not convene without government permission.

3. "Line up the government speaker at the opening ceremony." The Minister of Education had chosen next week to leave for Addis-Ababa. No conference there, but rumors of a girlfriend. Would the Minister of Agriculture agree to preside at the opening? Would the Prime Minister find a world conference of development economists important enough to visit? Though Ben knew neither of them personally, their staffs had some bright university graduates to write speeches that would not bring shame to the country.

4. "Check on the simultaneous translation equipment." Did the Ministry of Tourism offer it? Would theirs work? If it had to be flown in from Europe, the customs clearance would take days.

5. "Arrange hospitality." Would the guests like the accommodations? He had insisted they stay at an old colonial hotel in the city instead of a foreign one near the airport. He wanted visiting economists to walk through a historic African city to get a real look. He also wanted them to spend their money in national businesses and not foreign-owned ones. With its staff, some of whom had served since European colonial rule, the hotel would meet the competition in food, comfort, and entertainment. The tropical garden was splendid, but the noise of traffic or room air conditioners might be distracting. There was no swimming pool, and they might think the beach was not clean and safe. He would be dismayed to have a mass defection to the American hotel.

At the village development projects there would be no problem. Send them a pickup truck the day before loaded with beer, soft drinks, and blocks of ice along with some money to pay for a cow. By the next day the village would assemble to prepare the feast and entertain guests. African hospitality was alive and well there.

The problem came in the cities. Would the university student aides be helpful, well-mannered, and would they keep the guests out of trouble? He had requested a dozen of them from the University. Would the Italian delegate who liked to paint nude models make passes at the aides? The Asian who got arrested in a bar brawl in Chicago was coming too.

6. "Arrange the payments." The shift of site from Nigeria had cheapened accommodation costs to offset higher airfares. The bank drafts he was carrying would settle hotel bills reasonably. The problem arose with miscellaneous expenses. Many African delegates needed dollars, not checks drawn in local currency, so they could pick up books and equipment unavailable at home. The tour operator also demanded payment in dollars in order to smuggle in foreign equipment and luxury goods. The national bank would release only national currency, not dollars. The Ministry of Finance wanted to monopolize foreign currency for national priorities, which sometimes included ministerial junkets overseas. Though an economist would recognize that a hundred foreign visitors would bring in U.S.$70,000 in a week, the equivalent of the average annual income for 250 Miserians, the government would not agree to a foreign exchange account for the conference so that some dollars could be used for foreign expenses.

A former university economist met with the planning committee at his home and advised them confidentially to bring the cash in undeclared, since it would be less complicated that way. Ben was nervously carrying a money belt with ten thousand dollars in cash, a sum that represented a fortune on the parallel foreign exchange market in Miseria.

As Ben drank his morning tea, the captain announced they were preparing to land. A glance at his watch indicated the time was forty minutes before scheduled arrival. His stomach tightened as he realized that the local arrangements committee might not be on hand to welcome him and whisk him through Immigration procedures with his hidden, undeclared cash.

On the ground at 7:00 A.M., the hot humid air enveloped him as he descended the plane's staircase. He was back in Africa again. On the way to the arrival lounge he squinted in the sunshine looking for familiar faces at the entrance to the terminal or above on the visitors' deck. No one was waving at him.

In the arrival lounge, he waited his turn with the Health Inspector. Beyond him were the Immigration officials standing by cubicles for body searches. The next obstacle would be the Bank of Miseria, followed by Customs, where they would surely ask about the portable videocamera for the conference and try to charge heavy customs duties.

Ahead of him a European was held up for lack of a yellow fever shot certificate. He protested ineffectively as the Health Inspector led him off to quarantine. Poor fellow. He would run the risk of an unsterilized needle and spend a week at the airport waiting for the shot to take effect. Ben wondered who would be the next one pulled out of line.

He tried to look respectable but not noticeable, so the officials would dismiss him quickly. Most Miserian citizens were going through the inspection cubicles, unless they were friends of the officials. The father and son from Santiago Import-Export were talking excitedly with some officials. Still, no sign of his welcome party.

The Health Inspector waved him on to the Immigration official, who started thumbing through his passport. Looking up he said, "Where is your visa?"

Surprised, Ben responded, "What visa? I came three months ago to plan an international conference and none was required. My entry and exit stamps from the last trip are there."

The official looked at him and said sarcastically, "From Kenya you need a visa."

Ben realized he should not make a scene there, so he replied, "How can I obtain one on Saturday?" The official waved him to the side and ordered him to wait for the Chief Inspector. Ben relaxed a bit realizing that his welcome delegation might now arrive before the Chief. No such luck, though. The Chief came promptly, took his passport, led him to a room, and sat him on a hard bench next to a bedraggled Asian. Then he tossed the passport in a file drawer and locked it. He left them under the surveillance of a policeman calmly enjoying a cold soft drink while the sweaty Asian squirmed. The automatic weapon pointing at them on the policeman's desk made clear who drank in that office and who did not.

Behind the policeman blinked a video terminal. If it linked up to a database at the Security Branch or Interpol, the Chief could check their identities instantly. But no one was interested in verifying their identities. Ben wondered if they wanted a bribe. If so, they could dismiss the Asian and ask for it.

After a long period, Ben decided silence would cause suspicion. He asked the Asian, a young man wearing a dirty T-shirt and carrying a guitar case, "How long have you been here?"

"Two days," the man replied.

"Why did you come to Miseria?"

"I come from Singapore to Europe."

"But Miseria is not on the route to Europe!"

"I go to Kenya. No visa. They send plane to Miseria."

Poor fellow. Did he not have a European visa? Had they robbed him of his money? Did they accuse him of drug trafficking because of his looks? Did his loved ones or the embassy know where he was? Why did he not have the sense to know that no official would respect him dressed like a hippy?

"I come from Kenya," Ben answered. "Did you visit Kenya?"

"No, airport only," was the reply.

Ben asked the policeman in Spanish if he could go wash up. The man ignored him. For lack of response, Ben returned to his own thoughts.

Finally, the Chief Inspector returned. He had no interest in checking the video screen. He turned brooding eyes on Ben and launched into a harangue. "In Kenya your officials treat our people badly...."

So national revenge was the motive! Ben answered sympathetically, "My Miserian students tell me they are mistreated by the authorities of my country. I ask them to notify me of their arrival, so I can make inquiries if they do not clear Customs promptly."

The Chief was not deterred. "Why don't you intellectuals change the policies?"

"Protests by university students or lecturers are not appreciated by our government, as you know," replied Ben coolly.

The Chief smiled and asked, "What is your subject?"

Ben relaxed now that politics was no longer an issue. "Economics."

"My son studies economics at the University of Miseria."

"He must be intelligent and hardworking to have advanced so far," smiled Ben. "Does he know Professor Hudunu?"

"Yes," replied the Chief, his grin widening.

"Professor Hudunu should be meeting me at the airport for the World Economics Association Regional Conference."

"My son told me he will be employed at the conference."

"Good," said Ben. "We plan to have university students serve as aides to meet the delegates and observe the proceedings. The conference will then help to train future African economists." He paused. "But what can I do about obtaining a visa for this important conference?"

"Don't worry, I will give you a receipt for your passport until Monday, when my son will deliver it stamped to you. Welcome to Miseria, Dr. Mchunguzi."

"Thank you, Chief Inspector. You have helped us a lot."

The Singaporean squirmed on the bench while the Chief filled out the passport receipt. Though he had the opportunity to slip Ben a note for home, he did not move. Ben was too preoccupied with his unexpected good fortune to pay attention to the other's plight.

"Don't stay out after curfew or go out of the capital," said the Chief. "The military roadblocks will not honor anything but a passport. Now I will see that they let you through Customs."

Ben's relief was genuine. The arrival lounge was quiet now. His two suitcases sat by the customs table. In the Chief Inspector's presence the national bank employee quickly changed his hundred-dollar minimum for a tourist visit into five hundred Miserian bars, the local unit of currency named after the iron bars used in early trade with the Europeans. The Customs inspectors did not even leave their card game. They summoned a porter. Ben shook hands gratefully with the Chief Inspector and followed his suitcases out the gate. He looked at his watch. It was nine-thirty. He could still accomplish something this morning.

The next obstacle was the pack of taxi drivers. No welcome delegation in sight. Were they back in town phoning to find out about him? He asked the drivers in Spanish how much they would charge.

"Thirty bars, sir."

"Do I look like a tourist? You take Miserians for two bars."

They laughed and answered, "But we pick up more on way. We carry you direct."

"Fine, ten bars and you take me alone," answered Ben. "Twelve bars with those bags," a tall one answered. "Anyone say 'ten bars'?" No answer. He was dealing with a cartel and did not have the patience to break it down. "Does your taxi have good brakes and air conditioner."

"All fine!" said the driver with a big grin. "We go."

Ben paid the porter two bars, a morning's wages. The taxi's fine brakes were demonstrated as it stopped suddenly when the Taxi Inspector whistled it to collect a tax of two bars. The air conditioning, however, only blew out hot air, so Ben left the window open and looked at the countryside.

A patchwork of small farm plots went to the fence of the airport. Without stopping, the cultivated land continued through gaps in the chainlinks and extended around the hangars. He asked the driver, "How do those farmers plant in the airport security zone?"

"No problem! It their land before white man build airport. They still use it."

"Do thieves go through the fence and steal from the airport?"

"No. Airport workers know all those farmers, so no problem."

"Suppose some bandits hide in these fields to attack the airport."

"Don't worry! Villagers have charms in the fields against robbers and murderers, so none go there."

Ben did not worry, but wondered what trained mercenaries and terrorists thought of the charms. Still, mercenaries would insist on reconnoitering, and the villagers would spot them and raise the alarm even before an attack. Ben relaxed in the security of a society where everyone is known by his or her relationships. That security enabled Ben to enter the country without a visa on the strength of his colleague's student's father's trust.

A checkpoint appeared ahead. Several cars and buses were

stopped by uniformed men. "Is that the army?" he asked the driver.

"No, Customs. They check baggage. You in hurry? Give me ten bars and they let go." Ben thought of his passport receipt, hidden cash, and the videocamera and handed the driver a blue bill. The driver saluted the official revealing the bill in his right palm. They shook hands and the taxi passed the other vehicles.

The four-lane highway into the city was properly built but not well maintained. In low spots the storm drains had backed up, and the water undermined the asphalt. There the driver had to pick his way through potholes and then speed up again over the next hill. The interchanges were built for private cars. Private buses blocked traffic at each junction while passengers embarked and disembarked, loading and unloading baggage on the roof, surrounded by hawkers. The taxi plunged through the crowd honking its horn.

They passed the Presidential Palace, where army tanks stood guard while their crews relaxed under tarps stretched from the back. With their help the President could escape to the airport within minutes in case of trouble.

In the city an eight-foot wall covered with political slogans of the ruling party hid the slums from the road. Whitewashed dabbings efficiently covered any graffiti but left the slogans with unintended blanks in them. "One country, one leader" had become "One...one leader."

The taxi passed the sports stadium built by China, the central market given by USAID, the Roman Catholic Cathedral built in Spanish style.

Ben discreetly slipped his money belt into a bag that locked with a key and checked his watch. Five miles in half-an-hour with light traffic on the highway. It was ten o'clock when he arrived at the Grand Hotel.

He paid the driver twelve bars plus a one bar tip and thanked him for bringing him safely. He wanted an honest man to make more than the officials had charged on the highway. He could afford to be generous. Such incidentals would be paid with his expense account.

The reception clerk of the Grand Hotel recognized him and gave him the Royalty Suite for the conference. He deposited the locked bag and videocamera in the hotel safe. The old porter deferentially hurried to his suite in expectation of a substantial tip. Two bars did not thrill him, but he did not complain either.

The suite welcomed him with orchids on the coffee table, wicker furniture, high ceilings, a big brass bed, a huge bathtub with claw legs, a bidet, and a large verandah overlooking the ocean. The only flaw was an air conditioner that growled in the window.

Ben tried to call Professor Hudunu, who was still not in. He removed his suit, rumpled with all-night travel and sweat from the airport. He showered, shaved, and dressed in an African shirt, tropical slacks, and sandals. He felt like a man reborn.

As he checked Friday's newspaper, a messenger arrived to announce that students had come to meet him in the lobby. He chuckled remembering that the government-owned newspaper, the *Daily Flag,* was called by students the "Daily Rag," referring to its usefulness in the city's latrines. It never contained any information critical of the government, though plenty about opposition groups, such as intellectuals. It served to verify for him that the Cabinet Ministers had not changed.

He went to the lobby to see the students. He introduced himself and shook the hands of seven young men and five women. The son of Chief Inspector De Almeida was among them. His chubby face and shrewd eyes made him easily recognizable. Hudunu's daughter, Ilena, did not resemble her father. She was light-skinned with narrow eyes. Ben wondered if her mother were Ethiopian, Mauritanian, or from somewhere between in the Sahel.

Hudunu had chosen them well. All of the students spoke good English and Spanish. Four of them claimed to speak French too. One, who was Muslim, had learned Arabic in Quranic school. They all spoke several African languages as well. They would not have difficulty communicating with the conferees. They also dressed neatly, spoke politely, and gave no sign of dissolute habits that might encourage trouble during the conference.

Ben showed them the hotel ballroom that would serve as conference assembly hall. He indicated that two would sit at the head table to help the recording secretary and the simultaneous translators, two would stand at the side to pass messages and run errands for the delegates, two would stand at the door to verify identification and check umbrellas or luggage, and two would stay at the conference office to staff the phones and type. The other four would observe the conference and relieve the eight in their duties. Ben also explained their duties during conference registration and told them to return Tuesday morning at nine o'clock to find out about the delegates' arrival schedule and to lead walking tours for those present before the conference opened Wednesday afternoon.

The briefing over, he dismissed them with a handshake and returned to his suite. He tried to phone Hudunu again, but no one answered. He lay down and read drafts of manuscripts for the conference.

The first manuscript criticized the structural adjustment programs (SAPs for short) in Africa of the International Monetary Fund. A Frenchman, Philippe Petard, complained that cuts in government budget deficits to conform to IMF requirements occurred at the expense of basic social services. Health care and education were important investments for the long-run growth of African countries. Programs to mitigate the effects of SAPs were minimal. The commentators at the conference would no doubt have plenty more examples for this study.

Another manuscript, by a Nigerian, had a daring thesis. The author, Victor Vodumanyon, had calculated the present value of the services of nuclear waste disposal in scarce, geologically sound sites, which demonstrated that they were more valuable than Africa's richest mineral resources, even its gold, diamond, copper, or uranium mines, and rarer than low-sulfur petroleum. He then proposed that the services necessary to properly safeguard the nuclear waste disposal could represent a high technology industry for some of Africa's most backward economies. He acknowledged that the heads of African governments meeting at the Organization of African Unity in 1988 had banned all imports of toxic waste. And the 1989 Basel Convention on the Control of Transboundary Movements of Hazardous Wastes and Their Disposal required governments exporting toxic waste to notify receiving governments and to obtain informed consent. Still, he argued that they were passing up a very lucrative and economically sound opportunity.

Ben wondered if Dr. Vodumanyon planned to bring a bodyguard. He would need one if some of the conferees living in cities where foreign toxic waste had been secretly dumped started blaming him.

A third manuscript criticized the World Bank report "Subsaharan Africa: From Crisis to Sustainable Growth." Karla Curmudgeon raised questions about the report's bias in favor of Western business interests. After his experience with Miserian bureaucracy that morning, Ben was struck by the report's introduction:

A root cause of weak economic performance in the past has been the failure of public institutions. Private sector initiative and market mechanisms are important, but they go hand-in-hand with good governance — a public service that is efficient, a judicial system that is reliable, and an administration that is accountable to its public. A better balance is needed between the government and the governed.

Every conferee would have a well-rehearsed speech on Africa's economic adjustment to the debt crisis, and only lunch would bring relief. Ben was already hungry in anticipation of the end of that debate.

He returned to the lobby at noon to find the students still waiting there. The university van had not returned to pick them up as expected, and they would miss lunch on campus. It was two miles in the heat of the day to the bus depot and four to the University. Only one taxicab was on hand. Ben realized the snack bar at the hotel would overcharge them for lunch, so he handed them a twenty-bar note and told them to go to the road to buy from women food sellers catering to passersby and hotel employees. With that he turned to the dining hall to eat his expensive, prepaid European dinner as would befit the VIP organizer of an international conference.

Samuel, the senior waiter in a starched white jacket, greeted him and held his chair. As he ate his appetizers, he noticed a commotion out on the beach. Several people stood by a figure lying far out on the sand dune. Three policemen arrived in a Landrover. Onlookers appeared from all sides. Finally the crowd moved toward the hotel. As Ben tried to determine the cause of this activity, a police inspector arrived at his table and asked Ben to follow him.

Ben was surprised at this intrusion, but excused himself to Samuel and followed the official to the lobby. There he saw Ilena Hudunu and an older lady sobbing. "What happened?" he asked.

"My father has been killed."

Ben stood frozen. "I'm sorry. This explains why I have not been able to reach him. When was he killed?"

"This morning on the beach."

"How terrible!" Ben noticed her resemblance to the older woman. "Is this your mother?"

"Yes."

"Señora, my condolences for the loss of a dear friend!"

Just then the police inspector returned with the hotel director, two waiters, and a desk clerk. He ordered all of them into a police van in front of the hotel. The Hudunu family rode away in their own car with a policeman. As he prepared to enter the van, Ben spotted the students again with young De Almeida among them. He asked the police inspector if they were going to the Central Branch. He then told De Almeida to phone his father and ask him to call the Central Police Branch to verify Ben's presence at the airport during the morning.

The inspector rode with them in the van. The waiters started an African funeral song, and everyone joined in the chorus. At the Central Branch they went to separate rooms for interrogation.

A thin young police captain came in accompanied by a policeman with a notebook. "Dr. Mchunguzi, I am Captain Sodunu. My associate is Corporal Sojinu. I have some questions to ask you." Though his manner was crisply polite, his eyes did not veer from Ben's face. "Your full name, home address, place and date of birth?"

"Dr. Benjamin Mchunguzi Maluum, 103 Kensington Street, Apt. 301, London; born Nairobi, June 1948. My parents did not know the day of birth when they registered me to go to grade school."

"I understand. What organization is holding your conference?"

"The World Economics Association based in London is holding its African Regional Conference here beginning Wednesday evening."

"What is your role?"

"I am program secretary of the African Region on leave

as Senior Lecturer in Economics from the University of Nairobi."

"What was to be Hudunu's role in this conference?"

"He headed the local arrangements committee and would have chaired panels on 'Teaching Economics in an African Context.' "

"Which speakers were on his panel?"

Ben began to fidget. "We submitted our complete program to the Ministry of the Interior in our request for a permit for the conference."

Captain Sodunu responded coolly. "I have your request. Now I want to know what you truly intended."

"As I remember, Benito would give a paper comparing economics test scores of university students in Africa and Europe, Chakrabarty would present a project to write an Indian textbook treating underdeveloped countries as the norm and industrial nations as the aberration, Mbungu would discuss results of teaching economics in seminars for government officials. . . . " Fortunately, the subject matter of the panel would not arouse police suspicions.

"How did you meet Dr. Hudunu?"

"We attended a summer graduate seminar at Yale University in Connecticut, USA, on economic integration in Africa. He came from Columbia University in New York, and I went to Indiana University. We also had a hotel room together five years ago for one week at a World Economics Association Conference in Berlin."

"East or West?"

"West."

"When did you meet his family?" He already knew that Ben had recognized them.

"I met a daughter today and another son during my visit three months ago when I came to meet the local organizing committee."

"Do you know other members of the Hudunu family?"

"I do not know other Hudunus."

"Who were the members of the local arrangements committee?"

"Dean Gomez of the National University, Dr. Dossou in the economics department, and Assistant Minister Bongo of the National Commission on Higher Education."

"Did Dr. Hudunu have disagreements with any of the other members of the organizing committee?"

"None that represented a major problem. Dossou wanted us to meet at the American hotel because the facilities were more modern. The others favored a national hotel. No one suggested any members had an ownership stake in either hotel. Dossou gave in gracefully. Bongo wanted us to invite a government official to preside each day, but the rest decided that politicians would talk too much and not leave time for our work."

"What budget did Hudunu's committee have access to?"

Ben tried not to show his concern. "We submitted a budget to the Ministry of the Interior."

"Please be precise."

"The budget included 24,000 bars: 2,000 for expenses of university student aides; 3,000 for organizing visits to village development projects; a maximum of 7,000 for translation equipment, if locally available; 2,000 for photography services; and 10,000 for the final banquet."

"What about honoraria?" the inspector added. The man knew his job.

Ben winced but decided to be as frank as possible. "Our association commissioned four papers by African economists for this conference. The research and writing were done outside Miseria. They must be paid in currency that is acceptable outside Miseria, in our case U.S. currency. We applied to the Ministry of Finance for a foreign exchange account and were refused. As a result, we must pay them in dollars outside the official system. Otherwise, we could not commission papers for our conference. We also have two translators coming, who must be paid in dollars."

"How much money is involved?"

"Eight thousand dollars."

"Where is it?"

"I have it at the hotel."

"In cash or checks?"

"Cash. I must pay cash because African economists face exchange controls when they need imported equipment and supplies."

"Do they? Really!" His sarcastic reply turned coldly businesslike. "Who knew about the plan?"

"Myself, our accountant in London, and Hudunu. Asaba in the Ministry of Finance knew we faced a foreign exchange problem but did not know the sum involved." He did not mention Rosa, who would get the remaining two thousand dollars for her services.

"Someone in this country might kill for eight thousand U.S. dollars." He looked pointedly at Ben. "When did you arrive in Miseria?"

"This morning."

"On the 7:40 flight from London?"

"Yes. I stayed in Immigration until 9:30 A.M."

"Who was the officer who detained you in Immigration."

"Chief De Almeida."

The police corporal handed the captain a note that had arrived earlier. Captain Sodunu glanced at it and then back to Ben. "I see De Almeida phoned to say you were there until after nine o'clock. By that time the waiters had spotted Hudunu on the beach, though they did not know he was dead. Why did De Almeida phone here?" he asked warily.

"His son is a conference student aide at the hotel, so I asked him to contact his father on my behalf."

"Thank you, Dr. Mchunguzi. We will check your story and contact you if necessary. Please let us know before you change lodgings." He smiled professionally and shook Ben's hand. "You are free to go now."

Ben shook hands with the police corporal and left the room. In the hallway he looked for others from the Grand Hotel, but saw none. Outside the Central Station he caught a taxi. A block away he spotted the uniform of a hotel waiter at the bus stop and offered him a ride back. The man was surprised and grateful.

"Thank you, sir!" he exclaimed. "I go back soon now. Hotel no pay when I go police."

"I am sure when you are helping the hotel it is different from when you have personal problems with the police."

"I don't know. I don't like police." He shuddered as if in physical pain.

"Did they beat you this time?"

"No, they ask lot of questions."

"Did you answer with the truth?"

"Yes, I want no trouble!"

"Good! I hope the other waiter did too."

"Yes, they want to blame us little ones, not big ones."

"Like the hotel guests, who can talk to lawyers — and ride in taxis."

"Police know big ones have power. They have every-thing."

"Professor Hudunu was a big one, because he worked at the University. Did big ones kill him or did little ones?"

"I think little ones do not kill with a knife like that."

"He was killed with a knife?"

"Yes. It was terrible! Much blood there in the sand. If the hotel does not buy powerful charms, we all be cursed! One little hole and his lifeblood spilled out."

"So there was no machete from a farm?"

"No. A knife, from a kitchen. Once in the back! Who do it? Blood curse on him."

"A robber?"

"Man had swimsuit and towel only. What money for robber?"

The taxi driver was now interested, so Ben asked him, "Do robbers use knives and kill?" With his back to his passengers, the driver had good reason to know the habits of robbers.

The driver answered emphatically, "Why? Robber cover face. Lift machete. Take money and clothes. No kill at all!"

"You believe only big ones kill him?"

"I think so," they both answered in chorus.

The doorman looked surprised to find Ben and the waiter together when the taxi arrived.

When Ben picked up his room key, there was a message from the hotel director to come to the office. He was ushered down past the front desk into an extravagantly decorated room. The air conditioning was cold, so the director could wear his suit and tie. Walls were in dark African hardwood. Indirect lighting gave the room a mysterious glow. Behind a large desk sat the boss. His dark skin was set off by a charcoal gray suit and starched white collar. "Come in. I am glad to see you," he said pointedly. "How are you, Ben?" They shook hands.

"Not bad, considering my scrape with Customs and police and losing my friend on my first day here. Thank God your hotel is restful! I will need it. How are you, Musa? And your family?"

"We defend ourselves," he answered a little boastfully. "Sorry about Hudunu. Africa does not need to lose any more good men. Or women either," he added glancing at a diminutive, middle-aged African woman with fake red hair curled in an armchair in front of him. "You remember Rosa?"

"Of course! Good to see you again," he answered, glancing toward her and reaching for her hand. "We are counting on your excellent catering skills for the conference. I had planned to see you immediately but have been a bit pre-occupied."

She nodded and they both laughed nervously. "I am glad you are here, and I look forward to serving the distinguished visitors." Wearing a stylish blue African shift that hung off one shoulder, she looked like an Egyptian goddess. If her temper got mean though, she was more like an alley cat. Ben made a mental note to save enough time to talk to her at length and get the agreements in writing. She paused for effect. "I will miss Hudunu."

"We all will," agreed Musa. "I trust you are comfortable in the Royalty Suite, Ben?"

"Very. I look forward to enjoying it when I get the time."

"Stay for a week after the conference. It's free for distinguished visitors. We do not get as many now that the Americans are out at the airport." His hands chopped the air as he talked.

Ben tried to change the subject. "Do you still love American football?" Mr. Musa, who was built more like a jockey than a football player, had been a big fan ever since he had studied hotel management at Cornell University.

"I only get to see games when the U.S. Embassy invites me over for their game-of-the-week reruns each month."

"So you don't have a satellite dish on the roof?"

"The army would think we were spying. Finance would think we were wasting foreign exchange. Your intellectuals would call it 'cultural imperialism.' Only the Americans have a satellite dish. And I don't go there."

"Britain's *Punch* magazine once said that American football is the quintessentially American sport — random violence followed by a committee meeting." They all laughed. "So, do you have any advice for the conference?"

"We are glad you are here," said Musa sincerely. "It means a lot to me that you brought it here. We will do everything to make your conference a success. Just let me know what we can do."

"Me too," added Rosa from her seat.

"I'll see you later," said Ben and shook their hands again.

When he requested his room key from the desk clerk, he was dismayed to learn that the police had searched his room, but dismay turned to relief when he verified that the money in the hotel safe had not been touched. He asked for his money sack, returned to his room, and hid the two thousand dollars for Rosa under the well-worn soles of his jogging shoes.

He then inspected his files and belongings to see if anything was missing. Before leaving for Miseria, he had combed his files for anything politically compromising. Since some documents were out of place but not removed, he presumed the searchers must have found nothing or brought a portable photocopier. Much relieved, Ben returned the eight thousand dollars in cash to the safe at the front desk.

It was 6:15. He had not eaten a proper lunch and the formal European dinner in the dining hall would not begin until eight o'clock. He called for room service and ordered a plate of rice, African-style chicken stew in tomato sauce, and local beer, which he enjoyed on his verandah. Though it did not spoil his dinner, below him he could see the trampled place where Hudunu's body had been found.

He took stock of his situation. He had lost a friend. He could remember the good times they had together at Yale and in Berlin. Hudunu had other friends attending the conference. A circle of friendship had been broken by death. They would grieve together properly, and yet they could not delay an international conference to do so.

His thoughts were interrupted by a telephone call. Dean Gomez of the National University wanted to see him. Ben invited him up to the suite. They shook hands at the door. "How are you? And your family?" asked Ben.

"All fine, thank God," said Gomez. He had intense eyes behind steel-rimmed glasses and a shiny, bald forehead. "And you?"

"I and my family are well. Have you eaten?"

"Yes, my wife cooked for me," replied Gomez.

"Good African food, I suppose. Please, what can I offer you to drink?"

"Something to remember Hudunu with. Four corners?"

Ben telephoned room service to bring him German schnapps in a square-based bottle. It was now the standard brew used to pour out offerings to the ancestors.

While on the phone, the desk clerk informed him he was expected to attend Hudunu's funeral. The hotel van would leave at six o'clock to take him to the village. He protested that he could not travel inland, since he did not have his passport back from Immigration. The desk clerk assured him that the hotel treasurer would accompany him. At that point, Dean Gomez intervened to say that he personally would explain any problem to the soldiers. Out of respect for the Hudunu family, Ben agreed to travel. He asked for a wake-up call at 5:15.

Ben broke the seal on the schnapps bottle and poured a finger of alcohol into a glass. He then transferred the liquid to a second glass, as a gesture that both would drink from the same source. He added a finger of liquid to his own glass.

Gomez took the open schnapps bottle, looked out at the beach, and intoned, "Should we honor the spirits?" he paused. "O ancestors, we greet you. We bring you drink. Come and drink, ancestors." He poured a short stream out near the edge of the verandah. The sun-warmed tiles simmered the schnapps. The scent of alcohol rose from the spot. "We remember our brother Hudunu. We grieve at his passing." Pour schnapps. "We grieve for the widow and orphans from his untimely death. Ancestors watch over the family." Pour schnapps. "The ancestors conduct the fam-

ily safely to their village to commemorate their loved one."
Pour schnapps. "Ancestors watch over the colleagues and students of their son, Hudunu." Pour schnapps. Gomez spoke
intensely. "Ancestors, examine their conduct for any offense.
Ancestors, place the blood of the victim upon the murderer.
Come and drink, ancestors." He relaxed and handed Ben the
bottle only three-quarters full.

"Thank you. Do I make a prayer? In my country my family
does not make libation ceremonies for the ancestors."

"Pray as you wish." Gomez wiped his forehead with a
handkerchief.

Ben placed the bottle on the verandah and folded his
hands, as did Gomez. "Lord, our brother Hudunu is dear to
us. We ask that you take his spirit into your loving peace. We
ask that you watch over his family, colleagues, and students
saddened by his loss. We ask that in your wisdom you judge
his murderer. Abide with us in this time of grief. If his death
can lead others to find life in you, so be it. Amen."

"Amen," answered Gomez. He raised his glass, "To our
colleague." They both sipped.

The puddle of schnapps on the verandah had vanished, as
if someone had drunk it all.

Ben broke the silence. "Xavier Hudunu was a Roman
Catholic, and you, I believe, are a Catholic, yet do you invoke
African ancestors with libations?"

"His ancestors are Christians and so are mine. Don't you
believe in the communion of saints?"

"My grandparents are Christians too, but I do not think
of them as ancestors who mediate with the Creator. Perhaps I learned too much from the European pastors. For me
mediation is the role of Jesus."

"And the angels? They mediate too. And the saints and
heavenly hosts? Some visions in the Bible are like our African
traditions." Gomez laughed and changed the subject. "How
did you know Hudunu?"

"We debated such questions when we roomed together for a month at a graduate seminar in the United States. At the economics conference in Berlin we roomed together too. I proposed Miseria for this conference in order to see him."

"Did you see him?" Gomez was not laughing now.

"No, he died some time before I arrived at the hotel."

"I am sure it is shocking not to see him. He spoke well of you. I am ashamed that my country welcomes an international conference this way."

"Violence occurs in other countries too."

"Yes, but when the news reporters come here to cover this conference, all they will write about is 'Murder in Miseria.' What is natural in New York and is unnatural here becomes 'African savagery.' "

Ben responded bravely. "My duty is to announce the news to the conference with the dignity due him. We must hold a conference that will be beyond reproach. Then our colleagues will remember Miseria for its fine welcome." The schnapps was having its effect. He could feel the rhythm of the breakers on the beach.

"Hudunu had a great interest in traditional African economies. I remember him declaring that Western concepts of price and markets could not analyze the complexities of African markets."

"Yes. He studied under the economic anthropologist Karl Polanyi at Columbia."

"Polanyi expanded economic analysis beyond exchange to include reciprocity and redistribution. Hudunu did not just follow him, though. He proposed economics based on a religious tie to land and people, instead of Western individualism. He favored a sort of primitive communism, though he was not a Marxist."

"Fortunately for him!" responded Gomez. "We could not tolerate Marxists in my university. In this country such people die young and lonely. Could he have written anything that would give someone grounds to murder him?"

"He sent me most of his articles before he published them. And he sent me comments and reviews afterward. He did not quote Marxists, so no one could accuse him of Marxism. Marxists criticized him because he did not incorporate class struggle into his analysis."

"Our students are not radical. I doubt any Marxist in Miseria would see him as important enough to liquidate."

"Would he have offended any business interests? One of them might hire an assassin."

"He had no political influence, and he did not publicly express any views on the modern business sector in Miseria. He did his research on traditional markets. The local agents for import-export houses might disapprove of his Gandhian ideas, if they ever read them."

"I would call it 'Buddhist economics,' in the Schumacher 'small-is-beautiful' tradition."

"Hindu or Buddhist!" Gomez laughed. "You object when I mix my African ancestors with my Christianity. Now you are proposing to mix religion with your economics."

"Adam Smith was a Presbyterian, like me, and he founded modern economics. Behind Adam Smith's image of the 'invisible hand guiding the market' was the Presbyterian belief that God's plan was to neutralize human sinfulness, greed, and power, through economic competition."

"We historians acknowledge the role of religion in human events, but I thought you social scientists tried to ban it in the interests of being objective."

"Without a fundamental belief in the orderliness of the universe, one cannot practice science."

"Physicists tell me the universe is relative."

"Probabilistic models are still orderly."

The conversation continued on this level until the bottle was half empty. Hudunu would be honored by such a wide-ranging dialogue. Ben felt warm and light-headed. It was very dark when Gomez formally asked to "find the path home." From the ocean Ben could sense an appeal to find the murderer.

Chapter II

Accept the Rhythm of the Drum

℘

B EN AWOKE AT 5:15 to a knock at his door. "Who is it?" he called as he put on a bathrobe.

"Breakfast, sir," came the reply.

He opened the door warily. The waiter rolled the breakfast cart into the room. It was an English-style meal with hot porridge, toast on a silver rack, marmalade, and tea or coffee. Ben asked to have it on the verandah and tipped the waiter. He swallowed his anti-malarial tablet and then ate breakfast looking out at the beach. He noticed that Africans were not passing along the beach, but only a few tourists.

Down the beach were coconut palm plantations. He knew some plantation workers and fishing families lived there. Those families would probably know each other. They might rob a stranger forcibly. They might take his clothes and leave him in bathing trunks, but they would never give him a towel. They would not shed blood unless a feud had started. Then they would employ a heavy machete and chop at their victim. They would not stab with a thin blade, unless they had military training.

From that direction a determined murderer could have come the seven miles from the American hotel, fording several creeks to kill Hudunu, and then have returned. The person would have risked being seen and stopped by the fishermen, who were concerned about burglary since they lived so close to the capital. In a jeep driving below the tideline the murderer could have passed without leaving traces in the sand. The fishermen would not have tried to stop an official-looking vehicle, though they would certainly have noticed it. The murderer would also have had to arrange a rendezvous with Hudunu on some pretext.

Another possibility was a hotel employee or guest. The police were in the process of investigating them. Ben might learn something more.

From the west anyone could venture onto the beach from the city shorefront. Some watchmen guarding businesses on that side might see a suspicious-looking stranger. One who looked normal would pass unnoticed. That was the most likely direction.

The murder motive would be hard to determine. Robbery perhaps? According to the taxi driver, a robber would not have killed him. To Ben's knowledge Hudunu was not involved in politics, except to the extent necessary to hold a job in the country's only university. Though he could have jealous colleagues, they would most likely settle their accounts with gossip, spells, or poison, but not blood. If Hudunu had any romantic affairs, he was very discreet. Besides, the lover's husband would first demand monetary compensation. Violation of a marriage is breach of contract between families. Only Europeans or Arabs would make it a matter of honor to kill the adulterer. Did he have any business dealings? In Miseria, business could become very dirty. The courts were not reliable, so contracts were not enforceable. An entrepreneur had to protect himself with powerful allies. In the modern business sector sometimes disputes were settled in blood. Did Hudunu have debts? Did he have business partnerships? Ben wanted to know.

He dressed in a dark safari suit and sandals. To prepare himself for a day in a village, he took a shoulder bag with camera, umbrella, water bottle, and copies of documents from the conference for reading. Arriving downstairs before six o'clock, he found the hotel minibus already filling up. Ilena Hudunu and three somber girlfriends took the back seats. In front of them were other city folk in mourning clothing, apparently kin. In the front row was Manga, the hotel treasurer. He motioned to Ben to join him. In the front passenger seat above the engine sat an uncomfortable-looking European. Three hotel employees busied themselves stowing sacks of imported corn meal, cartons of canned goods, and heavy luggage on the roof. They worked with the good humor of men on holiday.

"Did you awaken well?" asked the treasurer.

"Very well. And you?" responded Ben.

"Fine."

He patted Manga. "You added stomach. The hotel must be prospering."

Manga laughed. "We can eat even when foreign currency is lacking."

"But you have European guests?"

"May I introduce Professor Biggles from London. He teaches linguistics this year at the University. They pay in bars."

Ben extended his hand. "Dr. Benjamin Mchunguzi. Happy to meet you. Did you know Professor Hudunu?"

"I met him here. Very sorry to lose him. He seemed like a pleasant chap."

"How have you found Miseria? Is this your first stay?"

"Yes. I enjoy the University. It's a pleasant place. Good colleagues and students seem eager to learn. It's a pity the budget can't provide a better library and more research facilities. I suppose the country would have to sell its soul to a foreign power to get the money, though." Biggles had thick glasses and the stooped posture of an intellectual well acquainted with books.

"Professor Biggles is staying at the hotel until the University finishes renovating a foreign faculty bungalow for him," Manga explained.

"Yes. I shall miss the good cheer of your beach bar when that happens. I don't mind the isolation from London. It helps me concentrate."

"Well, enjoy the beach bar. Yesterday it was drizzling when I left London." Ben classified him as in the euphoric stage of cultural shock. It would soon be followed by depression, when he realized what he had lost by being here. If he found some strong local interests, he would be fine. Otherwise, he could lose himself in drink, blaming his problems on Miseria. "Have you been into the bush before?"

"Just to cycle to a village near the University. It seemed rather primitive. The people were surprised to see a white man on a bicycle."

"They can't imagine you ride for exercise and pleasure, when they ride by necessity. Even near the capital the distinction is sharp between modern and traditional life."

"Dr. Mchunguzi, what do your friends call you?" asked Biggles.

"My African friends call me 'Dr. Mchunguzi' and in America they call me 'Ben.'" He smiled. "You may call me either. I am used to it."

"I see. What does the name Mchunguzi mean?"

Ben noted with approval that he pronounced it correctly, as a linguist should. "The Swahili word means several things in English: observer, inquisitive person, or investigator. My given name in Swahili is Maluum, which implies an astute observer or careful investigator. Quite a good name for a social scientist, don't you think?"

"Yes, quite. Were you given it at birth?"

"Yes."

"And Benjamin?"

"At my Christian baptism."

"So you were the youngest brother in the family."

"Yes, the clever observer—youngest son."

Manga laughed. "Our African names always tell a story."

"So do traditional European names, such as Benjamin," observed Biggles.

"Really! Benjamin is a European name?"

"Well, a biblical name from the Hebrew people."

"Oh, I thought it was an African name, because it is in the Miserian-language Bible."

"They translated it from the original Hebrew."

"But our Bible says 'Musa' in place of 'Moses' and 'Ibrahimu' instead of 'Abraham.' "

Ben laughed and chimed in. "So does my language, Swahili. Those biblical names came through Arabic."

At this point the bus engine started and put an end to the conversation. The three hotel employees leaped on board and scrambled to find sitting room. The junior one was relegated to facing backward over the engine.

Manga shouted over the roar to Ben, "These fellows are going home for the day. They know the funeral will be a big social event."

"How are you planning to get me through the roadblocks without a passport or identity card?" Ben yelled back.

"No problem. Wait and see," answered Manga.

The bus roared west through the commercial section of the capital. Family-owned shops faced the street with apartments above and storerooms behind. Sleepy night watchmen prepared to leave for the day. Lights in kitchen windows revealed cooks already at work.

Beyond that appeared a residential neighborhood. Cement two-story houses surrounded by high walls attested to their owners' wealth and standing. As they passed they could see gardens with beautiful tropical vegetation hidden behind wrought-iron gates.

Another mile and slums appeared. Adobe walls crumbled where thatch and rusty tin sheets failed to protect from rain. Twisting alleys were filled with puddles and refuse.

At the outskirts of the city, the bus stopped at a gas station just before the road crossed a swamp on a levee. Waiting there was a hearse, the Hudunu's car, and a university bus. Swarms of young women selling roasted corn, french-fried yams, soft drinks, and cookies surrounded the vehicles. Hands reached in and out of windows as snacks and payments passed through. Then the cavalcade started off with the hearse in front.

At a bridge on the levee, police mounting a roadblock stood at attention as the cortege rolled through. Respect for the dead superseded any attempt at petty harassment.

The road zigzagged up a valley toward the central plateau. Thick forest covered the hillsides. Where the road cut through, the exposed earth was red and sterile.

Eventually most of the travelers fell asleep. Biggles wore tape recorder headphones to drown out the engine's roar. Suddenly a suitcase flew off the university bus and snapped open on the roadway. The hotel bus lurched to missed it. Students streamed out of both vehicles, hooting and insulting the bus drivers, but the appearance of Dean Gomez put an end to the commotion. The suitcase and its contents were gathered up and loaded back on the bus while the students returned to their seats. The delay permitted Ben to ask Manga, "Will future roadblocks be as easy to pass?"

"They will be this morning," came the reply.

On the plateau small fields of food crops broke up the forest. Families were out at work before the heat of the day forced them to seek shade. Mothers with babies sleeping peacefully on their backs bent over to cultivate with short-handled hoes. Young men with machetes worked in teams led by elders to clear new fields and harvest plants. Older children followed the example of adults. They all stood to watch silently as the funeral caravan passed.

The fields appeared as jumbled patches of cultivation. Corn stalks supported bean plants. Heaps of earth grew big ceremonial yams. Huge blackened tree stumps jutted from the soil where partial clearing and burning had left them. Oil palms with their heavy leaves dominated cleared spaces. Each plant complemented the other in its ability to catch the sun, conserve the soil, and provide for a year-round supply of nourishment. Only human labor could cultivate the complicated patterns of plants. Besides, tractor cultivation would be useless without removing the stumps.

Where the crops had depleted the soil, skinny sticks of manioc, looking like bamboo with an umbrella on top, stood as the last crop before the family abandoned the field to return it to the forest. In twenty years new vegetation would reconstitute the soil, and the process of clearing and planting could begin again.

The absence of cattle surprised Ben. He shouted over the engine to Manga, "Where are the cows?"

"No cows here. Too much tsetse fly."

"How do you get meat in the capital?"

"Cows walk from the grasslands in the north. They butcher the cows here before they die of trypanosomiasis."

"In Kenya we eradicated the tsetse fly in some areas."

"Not here. Neighboring countries have it too, so they would infect us. We have an international program to eradicate the black fly, which causes river blindness in people. If that works, maybe the tsetse fly is next."

"What kind of landownership do you have here?"

"Each clan in the village has land. If a family member needs new land, the family elder assigns a field to clear. The recipient farms it until the fertility is gone, then abandons it to the bush."

"Do you own land in your village?"

"My family owns land that I farmed before I went for my education."

"Can you return to the land you farmed?"

"Of course. I can go to my village near here and ask for land. But they will give me new land, not the old land."

"Suppose you built ditches to irrigate and drain the land, would you own the investments you make?"

"I am not sure. I do own the oil palms that I planted before, even if another family member cultivates the land under them."

"Do men or women do the farm work?"

"Men do the clearing and much of the field work. Women help in the fields and also tend their gardens near the village."

"In Kenya women do most of the farm work."

"In Miseria men do most of it. Women do most of the trading."

At crossroads where trails spread into the bush, small country markets stood with thatched stalls waiting for market day. Every fourth day women and men with head loads came on foot, bicycle, or truck to stock their stalls, to trade, and to gossip. Already they were on the road to the Sunday markets. Those on foot turned slowly with their head loads, their eyes rolling sideways to see if the oncoming buses would stop for them. Their animated conversations died at the sight of the hearse passing.

"See, most of the traders going to market are women," added Manga.

The caravan passed villages with square adobe huts topped with thatched roofs. Each compound consisted of several huts enclosed by a mud wall. Perhaps one building would have a corrugated tin roof. The earth in the compound was bare. In the enclosures women and children swept the yard, stoked the fire, and pounded heavy poles into wooden pestles to break down the grain for the noon meal.

"Why is the ground around the houses bare?" shouted Biggles.

Manga was surprised at the question. "To discourage snakes and insects!"

At the outskirts of a major town they encountered another military roadblock. Again, they passed through with the respect due the dead.

By nine o'clock the caravan turned off the national highway onto a provincial gravel road. The change woke up the passengers. Dust from the preceding vehicles obscured the view. Even with windows closed and air conditioning on, dust entered the bus and settled on clothing and luggage. Ben remembered trips on public buses back to his home town. Only the warm welcome on arrival could compensate for the uncomfortable travel.

Suddenly the bus slowed down. Along the side of the road people were moving toward town in their best clothes. Mango trees flanked the road. Compounds were numerous. They crossed a small bridge and entered the market town of Hudu. The bus came to a stop in front of a house in the town square. Everybody clambered down.

Outside the buses the crowd milled around the villagers. Ben met his friend Dossou of the economics department at the National University, who greeted him warmly. "How are you?" Dossou exclaimed. His plump cheeks made slits of his eyes.

"In good health."

"And your family?"

"They were fine when I left Friday. How are you?"

"I am well. And my family, too." He became serious. "We were shocked to hear of our colleague's murder."

"I was shocked, too, when I learned of it after my arrival."

A young man interrupted them and requested that they and Biggles accompany him to visit the Chief. They entered the gate of a prosperous-looking compound. Inside, the buildings were freshly whitewashed and the children well-dressed. A private car stood out conspicuously. The young man ushered the delegates into a central building that had two armchairs at one end and straight-backed chairs arranged in a rectangle. Dean Gomez was shown to an armchair, and the rest found places along the wall. They sat quietly while other professors and notables were sought to fill the chairs. Then the Chief, wrapped in a dark African mourning cloth, entered and sat in the other armchair. He shook hands with Dean Gomez, who began to present the group.

"Honorable Chief, we have gathered here from many countries: Benin, Cameroon, Ghana, Nigeria, Britain, Germany, Kenya, and Miseria, to mourn our brother and colleague, Professor Hudunu. We are very sad that he has been taken from us and wish to offer our condolences to his family and town. That is why we have come."

The Chief replied, "We too mourn in Hudu the death of our son, Professor Hudunu. We do not understand why his days ended so tragically." He paused to let his words soak in. "We are relieved to see people come from so far to mourn this son of Hudu. We ask that you find those who have assaulted him so they can come to justice. We welcome you on this occasion."

At this point the young man brought out a bottle of schnapps and handed it to the Chief, who broke the seal. A young woman appeared with a tray of glasses. The young man poured a shot of schnapps in one, transferred it from one glass to another, and then gave it to the Chief, who drank it. Then the young man poured a shot into each glass and solemnly served the guests. The guests sipped it. Ben took a sip and then discreetly poured libations on the cement floor. Even if this was some kind of communion ceremony, he did not want alcohol on an empty stomach. He noticed Biggles finished off his shot quickly.

Dean Gomez thanked the Chief for his welcome and they

shook hands. Well-wishers shuffled forward to shake hands with the Chief as others exited into bright sunshine.

The crowd moved across the street to the Catholic church. The Hudunu family proceeded to the front followed by the delegation from the Chief's house. Village youths shuttled chairs from the Chief's reception room to seat important visitors. The university students crowded into the pews or stood along the walls.

The church was small and freshly whitewashed. At the front of the church a large painting showed a triumphant Christ on clouds. He had a Middle Eastern tan. The holy crowd who awaited his coming represented a cross-section of African society in traditional and modern dress, men and women, farmers and bureaucrats, Moors, Syrian merchants, and a white man wearing khaki shorts. All looked healthy and well dressed.

The African priest appeared with his acolytes. The atmosphere was solemn. The priest wore a tan cassock with a cream-colored surplice draped over it. The surplice was cut in a curve, so when he spread his arms for the invocation it hung in a half-moon from his wrists. The funeral mass was conducted in the local language.

Ben thought of funeral services of other friends. A close colleague died in a bus accident on a dangerous road to his home village. Another was lost in a plane crash and the body never found. The family could not accept the loss. Before Ben was born a sister succumbed to malaria. A dear brother died of an infection as a young man. Mother would not be comforted. After that he was always fearful of diseases. So far no one close to him had been struck with AIDS. It was the old common diseases that took them, as they did throughout Africa. In graduate school in Indiana a student was shot in a robbery. Now a dear friend had been murdered in Africa. "God, have mercy upon us! Christ, have mercy upon us!" he intoned with the others.

The priest gave a eulogy in Spanish, which stressed Hudunu's strong religious faith and the fact that he brought his whole family to mass.

"Very true," thought Ben.

The priest also praised Hudunu for being a loyal nephew of the town Chief, listening to the wisdom of the elders, and offering counsel when appropriate.

Ben wondered if he had been more discreet in Hudu than in the University, where he spoke his mind freely.

The priest also preached about Hudunu's generosity in supporting the parish vehicle fund, church renovation fund, and civic progress fund. Although Ben admired the church interior, he doubted any of those funds represented Hudunu's major concern.

After mass Ben and Dossou followed the congregation to the Hudunu home. Behind the white cement wall topped with iron grillwork stood a modern villa. The yard around it was full of visitors already, so they moved under the tent erected outside the gate next to the road. Folding chairs were set up under it. Some students ushered them to seats near the gate. They were relieved to be outdoors in the shade where a breeze moved the air.

"Who are the other economics lecturers at the University?" Dossou asked Ben.

"Two others besides myself... and Hudunu. Dr. Stepan is an old Eastern European refugee from the 1950s, who came out with a United Nations project and stayed when the University opened after independence. He is old and so grateful to be here that we do not see him as a holdover from colonialism. Besides, he will retire soon. The other is a young Miserian, Zande, who was one of our best students. He finished his doctorate at the University of Dakar in international trade. Dependency theory has impressed him deeply. He preaches economic self-sufficiency and wants to re-orient trade toward other Third World countries. He has become the faculty radical challenging us for selling out to the Western consumer society." Dossou chuckled. "He has a fine mind and can become a good role model to students. If he stirs up trouble, though, he will wind up either in the government cabinet or in jail. Either way he will be silenced!"

"What is Dr. Stepan's specialty?"

"He is an expert in agricultural economics. He was so traumatized by Stalinist collectivization, though, that he tends to see all government agricultural policies as evil. His ideal is agricultural cooperatives."

"Was his United Nations project successful with traditional agriculture?"

"It collapsed after the foreign technical experts left and the government could not offer the farmers credit. He just blames the government or the capitalists."

"Did Stepan disagree with Hudunu too?"

"Of course, they both approached the traditional economy from different perspectives. But they muted their differences. Hudunu was respectful toward the old man. Stepan seems concerned not to anger Miserians, so he can get his pension."

"So he picks fights with you, the Nigerian foreigner."

Dossou laughed, "I guess so."

"Did he come today?"

"No, he was not on the bus or at the mass."

"Did he have military training?"

Dossou's eyes widened at the suspicion. "I don't know. I never asked him."

Señora Hudunu arrived with her children and passed down the line of chairs greeting the guests. The whole family was dressed in a dark African print heavy with reds and blacks that distinguished them from other mourners. Señora Hudunu's cheeks were wet with tears as she greeted Ben. He noticed that her eyeshadow had run, but she was oblivious to her appearance. Her children were subdued, though they seemed to be enjoying the company.

The Hudunu family continued inside the gate. A group of drummers approached, beating rapidly on hand-held drums and gongs. The sound attracted Biggles, who was accompanied by a student explaining the rhythms to him. "These are praise names for the Hudunu family. 'Hudunu, child of Hudu, who founded the town of Hudu. Grandson of liberator who saved us from Sodu. Nephew of Chief. Friend of white man. He studied secrets of white man in their own country far away. He shared white man's secrets with us, so we are powerful.' "

At these words people came forward to drop tips in the drummer's shirt pocket.

Ben listened intently to the student explain the rhythms, and he asked Dossou, "Does Sodunu mean 'Son of Sodu?' "

"Yes, why?"

"Sodunu was the name of the police officer who interrogated me yesterday. Would he be influenced by political rivalries with Hudu?"

"I would be suspicious if he were in charge of the investigation."

"How can we find out?"

"Ask Dean Gomez. He has contacts throughout the government."

The student returned and continued the drum translations. "He is drumming for that elder in the chair. That bleary-eyed drunkard loves to hear praises for his ancestors, whether they are true or not! Look, he stuck a five-bar note on the drummer's forehead. He wants us to think he is a generous big man, when he is only an old fool."

Ben asked the student, "Is he on the town council?"

"Yes. He represents a big clan."

"Do the young people in his clan respect him?"

"They must. It is tradition."

"But you do not?"

"I am polite. I do not show disrespect to him."

"Do you respect your teachers?"

"Of course! They share their knowledge with me."

"Does he have traditional knowledge to share with village youth?"

"They fear him as a witch."

"Do you believe he is a witch?"

"I no longer live in this village," the student answered evasively and moved away.

Ben looked at Biggles. "I am sorry. I may have discouraged your informant."

"I'll chat with him later. Drum linguistics is not my specialty anyway."

A woman appeared with a tray of glasses, which she distributed to people sitting in the chairs. Behind her a man held a whisky bottle reserved for distinguished guests. Biggles eyed it eagerly. Another young man carried a case of beer and one of soft drinks. He efficiently poured the liquid down the side of the glass until it was full to the brim without foam on top. Ben and Dossou selected beer, which was lukewarm. When people in the chairs had been served, there was a scramble among the hangers-on for the remaining bottles of beverage. The winners quickly found a spot of shade and passed the bottles to their friends.

Soon a girl arrived with a bowl of water, soap, and a hand towel. Each guest quickly washed the right hand to prepare for eating. Plates and forks were distributed. Young women individually served the first course of macaroni and tomatoes. Then they brought huge helpings of white rice topped with a serving of beef in peppery gravy. The groups of hangers-on got big basins into which large quantities were dumped. They squatted happily beside the food, eating with their right hands.

Ben, Dossou, and Biggles ate in silence like the others, listening to the drumming that continued in the courtyard. Ben marveled at how efficiently the Hudunu family was feeding three hundred or so guests. He remembered family celebrations in Kenya where multitudes were fed. He looked at Dossou, "The Americans have a saying: 'There's no such thing as a free lunch.' "

"They have never lived in a society where hospitality is the major virtue. 'As God gives, the family shares.' So we Africans recognize that even when there is scarcity, distribution is not based solely on ability to pay."

"There is a free rider problem, though. Any one can walk up and join the hangers-on," observed Ben.

"No, they can't. Those groups squatting there will not accept an unknown among them. They would insult and push the unknown person away."

"What about beggars? There are some in every town."

"They are known. They would be given their portion separately," answered Dossou.

"So you are saying a price system is unnecessary?"

"When people live in a traditional society with social controls it is unnecessary. Each family butchers a cow for a family ceremony and invites the others. The others return the favor. That is the principle of reciprocity at work. It also insures the distribution of meat throughout the society without use of refrigeration."

"You sound like Hudunu now. First, you justify African tradition on its own terms, then you point out its economic efficiency as well."

Dossou looked distracted. "It is easy to do that here in his ancestral home in the heat of the day after a big lunch and a glass of beer. Let's see if they have some place to take a siesta."

Inside the gate, groups were lounging under the trees after the midday meal. Even the drummers were relaxing with their friends. Dossou asked a Hudunu family member for a place to sleep. They were shown into the living room and given their choice of armchairs or reed mats on the floor. Other men were already dozing off. They loosened their clothing and lay down.

Two hours later Ben awoke slowly. In a world of clocks and air conditioning he would not have the luxury of time. Here his responsibilities for the economics conference seemed far away as he lay in the heat of the day. He would force himself to discuss local arrangements eventually. In the meantime the town of Hudu drew him into its world.

He rose carefully so as not to waken Dossou or Biggles and went out into the bright light. Under the trees he noticed a group of students among whom were some conference aides. He ambled over and greeted them. "Good afternoon."

Recognizing him, they replied in unison, "Good afternoon, Professor."

"I have some questions about the town of Hudu. Are any of you from here?"

"Yes," answered several.

"How was it founded?"

A self-appointed spokesman for the group explained, "My ancestor, a hunter from Sodu came and found that this was good agricultural land, so he brought our clan and settled here."

"What is your name?"

"Hudunu Felipe. I am the nephew of the Professor."

"How did your ancestor obtain permission to settle here?"

"The king of Sodu granted it."

"So he paid tribute to the king and received protection for his family?" They nodded. "How long ago did this happen?"

"When trade began with the white men."

"Was that the slave trade in the 1600s and 1700s or the tropical produce trade in the 1800s?"

"Tropical produce rose in the 1800s after slave ships were stopped by the British Navy. More products were exported from Sodu. So people were looking for more land to farm."

"How far are we from Sodu?"

"About fifty kilometers by dirt road. In the rainy season, when the road is impassable, people can use canoes on the river that the bus crossed entering town."

"So products from this land could be shipped downstream to an ocean port?"

"There are rapids, but there are portages around them."

"Does trade still pass through Sodu to Hudu?"

The students looked at each other and grinned. "No, not after the colonizers built a railroad from the capital. We built a connecting road to the railway station and freed ourselves from Sodu."

"Did Professor Hudunu's grandfather organize the road to the railway?"

"Yes!" they all answered in astonishment.

"Were the people of Sodu oppressing your town?"

"They insulted us and said that we were their juniors. They charged high prices to export our products and import manufactured goods."

"Was that because they were greedy or because their port was inefficient?"

"Both. And Hudu does not accept insults."

"Is there trade today between Sodu and Hudu?"

There was an embarrassed silence at this point, as the local students looked at each other. Finally, one answered, "The smugglers in Sodu trade with Hudu."

"What are they smuggling?"

"Tape recorders and videocassette recorders. The customs duties in the capital are very high."

"There is a principle I teach in my international trade class. If you set the taxes too high, government earns less, because smugglers find that ways to avoid them are cheaper than paying them."

"Professor Dossou tells us the same thing. But the Minister of External Commerce is from Sodu. He sets the tariff too high so his family can benefit from the smuggling," they answered triumphantly.

Ben looked around and saw Professor Dossou smiling at them. "I see you came out at the right time! I am impressed with your students. Now I want to see today's market. Will any of you accompany me?"

They volunteered eagerly, as did Dossou. When they were in the street, Dossou pointed out a bicycle with boxes of electronics goods perched precariously on the back leaving the market. "I suppose you think those are smuggled," he said with a grin. "Let's follow him and see where he goes."

Ben looked at the students, who were smiling too. "If it is done in broad daylight, I don't see why you were so reticent back in the courtyard." By now the bicycle had disappeared around the corner, but no one hurried to see where it was going.

Dossou explained, "We have an inventor in this town who discovered how to open up some electronic equipment and rewire it to run off car batteries. He does a thriving business on the next street. He also takes alternators and connects them to bicycle chains so villagers can recharge car batteries by pedaling. The market for used car parts is hot now too. We have to hire drivers to protect our vehicles when they are parked."

"It sounds like the social consequences of this invention are disastrous," observed Ben.

"I would not say that," answered Dossou. "Felipe, tell Professor Mchunguzi what happened in your village when they bought a video player."

"My brothers decided not to leave their village to go to the capital. They could go to the general store in the evening and watch movies just like at the cinema."

"How could they pay for them?"

Dossou replied, "A network of traders gets them from the Middle East. They copy them and rent them out cheaply.

The young farmers have extra land that they cultivate in cash crops to pay for entertainment."

"But how do the traders find the foreign exchange to pay for them?"

"By smuggling out cocoa and spices produced by the young farmers."

"So the government fails to receive customs duties and foreign exchange, though individual officials benefit from the illicit trade," Ben concluded.

They arrived at the inventor's house. It had a mud wall with a wooden gate. Inside, the courtyard was neatly swept and some women and children were preparing food. On seeing the visitors entering, they sent a child to summon the head of the household, who emerged from a room at the back wearing some baggy shorts and a T-shirt. He greeted Dossou and the others in the local language. They introduced Ben.

He smiled and said in stilted Spanish, "You are welcome. Very happy to meet you."

"Good to meet you," answered Ben.

He opened the door to a small reception hut and invited them in. Once beer and soft drinks were served and the libations poured, he asked Ben, "You come from far?"

"I come from Kenya. Professor Dossou said you can fix televisions and video players. That is very good."

"Fix what kind?" he asked.

Ben persisted, "Did a teacher show you how to fix televisions and video players?"

"I no go to school." Dossou interrupted to ask in the local language how the man learned to rewire electronic machinery.

"I work for Lebanese importer in capital. When televisions and video players are spoilt, he ask me fix them. So I ask friends who help me. And I find wires work on battery. Then the Lebanese leave. So I fix old television and sell to bar man in capital. He tell others and they ask me to fix also. Then police come and want taxes. So I leave to Hudu. My cousin,

Professor Hudunu, send me television and video player. I fix and sell. Then I fix and sell more. Now four apprentices work here."

Ben wondered if that was the way the industrial revolution began. The capital taxed invention and the hinterland applauded it.

"Thank you. I am glad to hear your story."

"You are welcome. Come again," replied the inventor pleased with the visit.

After each shook his hand, the group left. Once they were in the street again, Dossou asked the students, "Did you know about his inventions?" Some nodded affirmatively while others did not.

"Why doesn't he buy a car?" asked one student.

Dossou responded sternly, "How can he continue his business if he wastes his capital? And what would the police do if they found he had a car and no official income? He needs to accumulate capital and find a business partner who will build electronic goods designed for village use. That is what you intellectuals can do to help him. How would you redesign the equipment for Miseria?"

"Dustproof it," said one student as he wiped his face with his handkerchief. "And protect the circuits from this humidity."

"Stitch a cover for it using local materials," chimed in another.

"Add shock absorbers," said another, observing a bicycle rattling along the ruts.

"Make the components replaceable or repairable," answered another.

Ben smiled, "I am impressed by your students' inventiveness. But how are they going to pay for imported parts?"

"Export some of the equipment to neighboring countries," several shouted enthusiastically.

"And if they have exchange controls we will engage in

countertrade, our electronics exchanged for their manufactured goods that we want. Without use of currency."

The brainstorming continued all the way to the market.

In the market the stalls were grouped by products sold. Live animals were near the exit, so they would not disturb the other sellers. Bulk foods were near to the truck park so that they could easily be loaded again. Inside the market the women vegetable sellers were lined up together. Ben asked students to price eggs, tomatoes, pineapples, and yams. The women laughed good-naturedly when they heard an intellectual wanted to buy their products. "Send your wife," they called.

The houseware, hardware, and toiletry sections also had women sellers lined up next to each other. Each had brought one load on her head to market for the day. None was there to deal in wholesale quantities.

In the textile section Ben became serious, since he needed some African cloths for presents back home. A crowd formed as he dickered with two women sellers through student interpreters. After a few tense moments as the sellers insulted the students for siding with the rich foreigner against their own townsfolk, the women understood that Ben's relationship as teacher meant that the students needed to show him favor. Ben responded to their change of heart by complimenting the sellers on the fine selection. With that the negotiating atmosphere improved, and prices suddenly became reasonable. After bargaining, Ben bought a six-yard piece from each woman for the equivalent of forty U.S. dollars.

After the onlookers departed Ben continued to the medicine section to examine local remedies. There he found such things as anti-malarial drugs, penicillin vaccine, and syringes abundantly available in the hot sun of the market. Modern medical paraphernalia shared the stalls with roots, bones, leather amulets, brass rattles, and other traditional medical equipment. He asked if there were traditional medicines for sale that had been recently introduced. The seller pointed to some white stones and said they came from Europe. She could not tell him why there was no packaging on them. He asked what they were for, and she said they cured skin ailments. He asked the students in Spanish, "Could she could be selling an illegal drug, crack?"

They assured him, "The villagers know about local psycho-active plants. They use them in religious ceremonies. They would not import illegal drugs."

"Even if they are more powerful?"

"It would waste valuable foreign exchange."

The economic logic was compelling. Electronic goods could not be manufactured locally, so they were imported. Psychedelic drugs did not need to be brought into the county. Ben handed Felipe a ten-bar bill and asked him to purchase a plastic bag at another stall and then return and buy a small sample of the white stones. Ben did not want to be carrying an unknown substance himself without proper legal identification.

On their way out of the market they spotted Biggles. He was surrounded by a crowd watching with great interest while he tried to bargain through a student interpreter. "I hope his linguistics is serving him well," remarked Dossou.

During the walk back to the Hudunu house the students asked questions about higher education in Kenya, Britain, and the United States. Ben was frank with them about the cost of education and the limited scholarship opportunities for African students. He pointed out that the investment made in their education in Miseria was intended for them to develop their own country rather than to emigrate to developed countries. One brave one asked him whether he had emigrated to Britain, and he assured them that he and his wife and children intended to return to Kenya once his term with the World Economics Association was completed. His present responsibility was to organize professional training opportunities for economists within Africa.

Before they reached the Hudunu compound, they could hear a voice over the loudspeaker announcing gifts to the bereaved family. A tall young man, very dark, in a slim-cut European suit was pacing near the gate. He greeted Dossou and the students. Dossou introduced him to Ben as Dr. Zande of the economics department.

"I have been waiting to meet you," said Zande affecting the French accent of a Dakar graduate.

"Pleased to meet you," replied Ben.

"I hope all is going well with organizing the conference."

"I am afraid that I have not been able to since I arrived, because of the shock."

"Yes, we are all disturbed," agreed Zande. "Dr. Dossou, have you prepared the envelope?"

Dossou produced an envelope from his pocket with "From the economics department in sympathy with the Hudunu family" written on the front. Zande counted ten hundred-bar notes.

Ben was impressed. "You are going to give a month's salary to the family."

"Yes. It is not too great a sacrifice for his colleagues," Dossou replied. "His wife has all the funeral expenses and her widow's pension will not be enough to educate the children."

Inside the compound the crowd stood or sat in the courtyard looking at a table on the porch where the announcer with the microphone stood. People would go forward one-by-one to hand an envelope to Señora Hudunu and whisper some words to her. She would then pass the envelope to her son and an older family member who opened it publicly. They counted the gift and recorded it in an account book. Then the announcer declared to the whole neighborhood the amount of the gift. As the announcer called out sums of one thousand bars or more the crowd sighed in appreciation.

Ben was surprised at the generosity of neighbors who obviously earned very modest incomes. He remembered ostentatious generosity in Kenya at harambee celebrations designed to raise funds for community development projects. He knew that as representative of the World Economics Association he would have to give accordingly. He whispered to Dossou, "I only changed the minimum one hundred U.S. dollars at the airport. Can I give a check?"

"No. It would cost her money and trouble to cash it at the bank. Better give her some foreign exchange."

"It's illegal."

"Don't worry. They will change it on the parallel market."

"But if they announce it?"

"No. They will be discreet."

Ben stepped away from the crowd and slipped two crisp one-hundred dollar bills out of his money belt, put them in an envelope and wrote "In sympathy from Dr. Mchunguzi, World Economics Association." He followed Dossou and Zande up to the table. Dossou and Zande each shook Señora Hudunu's hand in sympathy. The crowd responded with appreciation to their gift of one thousand bars. Ben also shook her hand and said, "Señora, I am so sorry."

"Hudunu always spoke appreciatively of his friendship with you," she answered.

As he turned, the announcer declared that the World Economics Association through Dr. Chunguzi from Kenya had contributed 1,500 bars and the crowd cheered him. He was relieved that the announcer had calculated his gift in bars and noticed that there was a 50 percent premium on the parallel market for foreign exchange. It intrigued him to think that his gift would soon be purchasing smuggled electronics.

Dossou and Zande both told him he did well and that they were proud to be part of an organization that honored its members. Dean Gomez came over smiling and congratulated him on his generosity. "We Africans must show that when one family sorrows we all sorrow, and when one family is joyful, they share," he said, paraphrasing 1 Corinthians 12.

"I wanted to show my solidarity with his other colleagues," responded Ben. "When can we talk about the official arrangements for the conference?"

"I will pick you up tomorrow morning at eight-thirty. We have an appointment at the Ministry of the Interior to obtain our conference permit. Then we will inspect the translation equipment at the Ministry of Tourism. If it works, we only have to pay their technician to transport it. Also, I have contacted the Prime Minister's office about his opening the conference. We can get the answer tomorrow. If necessary, Assistant Minister Bongo of the Commission on Higher Education is ready to do it. That is the advantage of planning the meeting with him on the committee."

"I appreciate your preparations. If everything works, we are fine."

"God willing, we are fine." Gomez smiled again.

"Incidentally, the police captain who interviewed me about Hudunu's murder was named Sodunu. Is he in charge of the investigation?"

Gomez frowned. "I will check into that!" he replied. "In the meantime I hope you are enjoying yourself."

"I am happy to be here with you. In London I miss these trips to traditional Africa. I also enjoy conversing with my colleagues."

"Good. We are glad you are here too." Gomez left them to go talk with some local politicians.

Zande introduced Dr. Rivera from Puerto Rico, a visiting professor in the Fulbright Exchange Program sponsored by the United States.

"Pleased to meet you," said Ben. "What is your specialty?"

"Tropical forestry. Are you familiar with sustainable development?" He glanced challengingly.

"Yes, our conference commissioned a paper evaluating village development projects. We want projects to be sustainable, both in terms of protecting the environment and also ensuring the villagers can manage the project eventually, instead of depending on the aid agency."

"Suppose the self-interest of the landowners is to exploit their villagers and the environment?" asked Rivera distrustfully.

"I admit that in some countries in Africa we have landowners who may be so short-sighted. However, here in Western and Central Africa communal land tenure means elders are responsible for family land. They will not knowingly degrade the family legacy."

"In Latin America we have seen the most indebted countries sacrificing their forests to earn money to pay off the debt."

"That happens in Miseria too because elders see it as a way to clear land for agriculture."

"These attacks on the forest result from social class structure," Rivera asserted.

Ben looked at Zande and changed the subject. "What are the consequences of Miseria's proximity to an economic giant such as Nigeria?"

"When Nigeria coughs we catch cold," he replied, frowning at Dossou. "For a while our country tried to free itself from European influence by accepting Nigerian influence. The Nigerians built an impressive embassy to rival those of Spain, France, and the United States. We exchanged business and cultural visits. Just after our country finished negotiating accords to supply food and raw materials in exchange for preferential petroleum prices, OPEC lost control of the market. Our government abrogated the petroleum delivery contracts since the world market was lower than the agreed rate, and the Nigerians canceled their orders from our producers."

A young man approached and asked them to be seated for supper. Ben, Dossou, Zande, and Rivera found chairs. As at noon they were given a choice of beer or soft drinks. Then they were served corn mush covered with peppered fish stew and sauce of boiled okra, whose strands stretched from the pot to each plate. Dossou called it "telephonic sauce" because it strung wires between people.

Drumming began. One man led the rhythm on a gong. Four others beat drums ranging from small, hand-held ones to a large, immobile one made out of a tree trunk. Each drum took up a separate rhythm that the drummer wove in and out of the lead rhythm. Another man had a huge gourd with a small opening at the top. He struck the opening with a fan to emit a deep whisper that would fill silences between drumbeats.

Now that the microphone was no longer in use to announce gifts, some youths were attaching electric guitars to the public address system.

Students and town youth strutted out into the clear space in front of the drummers and began to tune their bodies to the drum beats. Their pelvises followed the gong, shoulders the big drums, and feet the small drums. Their heads remained still in the midst of the movement with no smile, just an expression of inner peace as they accepted the drums' rhythms into their bodies.

A rivalry developed on the dance floor as individual youth from the town or university performed movements and then challenged others to follow them. The town youth produced some impressive acrobatics, though the university students clearly had the smoother city movements. Both groups seemed satisfied with their performances and soon mixed easily.

When the drummers paused to rest, the guitar players started up some High Life rhythms that brought out city folk. Ben invited one of the friends of Hudunu's daughter to join him in the two-step dance. She accepted, but her heart was obviously elsewhere, and he felt relieved when the number was over. He turned his attention to a woman his own age who danced gracefully. During the break he learned she was a distant relative of the Hudunu's and a schoolteacher from the capital. She knew about him since her ride that morning with Dean Gomez and his wife. Her name was Teresa.

When the traditional drummers began again, the elder townsfolk came out to dance. Ben asked Teresa whether the rhythms were designed to invite them. She explained that the dance was old and complicated. Only the elders would perform it properly. Ben noticed that the gong did not maintain a basic rhythm, though the dancers seemed to perceive a hidden beat and patterned themselves together on it. They also used a sign language. Teresa explained that they asked each other riddles. They began each riddle with a challenge, "I have two eyes in the spirit world and two eyes in the natural world." She could not follow the riddles, though, because she came from the city.

Ben and Teresa drank beer while they watched the elders finish their dance and the young people reconquer the dance floor. This time Biggles ventured out to join them. He was a bit unsteady on his feet to begin with, and his body refused to accept the rhythm of the drum. It jerked back and forth on its own time. Students adeptly moved behind him to imitate his awkward movements and the audience laughed, and then applauded the strange white man. Biggles smiled and continued until he tired out in the middle of a song.

Time passed quickly as Ben and Teresa talked. Perhaps the conversation, perhaps the beer, perhaps the cloud of dust or dim lights from the porch made the dancers fuse together in one body with many legs and many shoulders moving together — around one central rhythm. Ben relaxed as that rhythm absorbed the pressures of his daily life. He found it was good to be back in Africa.

Toward midnight the music stopped, and the announcer informed the audience to prepare for return to the capital. Ben thanked Teresa for an enjoyable evening and invited her and her husband to attend the ball following the opening session of the conference. He thanked members of the Hudunu family for their hospitality, congratulated some of the dancers, and headed toward the hotel bus. Felipe, who had gone to buy white rocks for him, found him and handed him his package. With great commotion all the bus riders arrived back on board. In contrast to the morning they were chattering happily, even the Hudunu daughter and her friends. Manga bragged about how much he had eaten and congratulated Ben on his fine gift to the Hudunus.

"We must all help the family," Ben replied modestly. Then he whispered, "Will we have any trouble with roadblocks on the way back?"

Manga discreetly slipped him an identity card and whispered back, "You are now Elijah Abobo of Ibadan, Nigeria. Check your birthdate and parents' names."

Ben read the card and was shocked. "You have fake identification cards?"

Manga smiled. "No, real ones! He was a hotel guest who failed to pay his bill. We took the identity card when he went to jail."

"What will happen to him?"

"He will stay there until he repays the politician he tried to cheat on a bogus import contract."

Two young men brought a tipsy Biggles to the bus and helped him into his seat. He looked sick.

Ben tried to sound helpful. "The crowd enjoyed your dance."

"Tha waas soo loong agoo," came the reply.

The bus engine started, ending further conversation. Ben was relieved when he noticed that they would return in convoy with Dean Gomez's car and the university bus. He appreciated all the legitimacy they could muster for the roadblocks.

As the bus roared over the night road, other passengers slept, including Biggles. Ben slipped the bag of white rocks given him by the student into the lining of the seat in front of them. He remained vigilant lest he forget the facts on his identity card. On the main road at the first roadblock a soldier entered the bus and swept each face with his flashlight. He also looked briefly under the seats and prodded some packages. He checked the drivers' papers and then waved them through.

Manga breathed a sigh of relief. "I expected they might pull us off the buses. With this many young people they might fear some political gathering. There were probably some Special Branch agents on the university bus to make sure the crowd was not subversive." Manga went calmly back to sleep.

Ben thought back over his conversations with the VCR repairman and at supper in case he would have to answer for any political statements.

At the roadblock near the capital the soldiers on duty recognized university vehicles. They joked briefly with the bus driver and then let them through. Ben slipped the bag of white rocks back into his shoulder bag.

The bus arrived back at the hotel around three in the morning. Ben said goodnight to Manga and the university students and stumbled off to his room. He was delighted to return safely to his bed.

Chapter III

Near the Seat of Power

✂

BEN AWOKE FROM A VIVID DREAM. He had been dancing on the sand when a hole opened up between him and his partner. The two kept trying to dance, but they had to lean over the hole, which was getting deeper and wider.

He rolled out of bed and slipped into jogging shoes and shorts, resolving to work the travel strain out of his body. He tiptoed downstairs and out through the pleasant garden. The cement wall of the hotel had slats in it to let through sea breezes. He greeted an old watchman at the gate to the beach. Would he have seen anything suspicious Friday night?

Ben chose to run in the direction of the capital. No break occurred between the garden wall of the hotel and the wall of the commercial district, which was strictly functional: eight feet high and topped with broken glass and concertina barbed wire to keep prowlers out of the storerooms behind. The first two commercial properties had nicely whitewashed walls just like the hotel. After that the others looked weather-beaten and discolored. A sign on one threatened fines if anyone urinated on it. Brown parabolas below the sign indicated the threat went unheeded.

Behind the walls he could see windows with steel bars

where the business owners lived and worked. Steel doors were locked from the inside; the businesses opened in the other direction to the street.

After a quarter of a mile he came to a break in the wall where a train track left the business section and turned onto the beach. Some outhouses were strategically placed there. A prowler could leave the commercial district or the beach without drawing attention by pretending to relieve himself in one of those facilities.

The railway continued along the beach outside the wall for another mile. There it met other tracks and turned onto a jetty that extended out into the ocean through the line of surf. In the early morning small lighters were tied against the jetty, waiting for the sailors and stevedores who would move Miseria's exports and imports to and from the freighters safely moored out on the horizon. "So this is the port that supplanted Sodu," thought Ben as he turned around and headed back to the hotel.

His head clearer now, he remembered running as a boy on the mountain paths in Kenya. At that time he had never seen the sea. He never expected he would be organizing conferences on the other side of Africa and never realized what responsibilities he would have to face. Still, he was glad to be running on a new day, ready for the experiences he would face.

At seven he listened to the radio news to make sure no world events would affect the conference. He showered and dressed in a light suit and stylish European tie. Samuel, the old waiter, welcomed him in the dining hall, which was almost empty. "Good morning, sir," he greeted him.

"Good morning. How are you?"

"I awakened well, sir. I bring tea or coffee?"

"Tea."

"You take continental or order breakfast?"

"Continental."

"Over here," Samuel indicated the buffet.

Ben chose from a selection of rolls, butter, jam, and cheese. He was annoyed that the food style and brands all came from Europe. At least they offered some local tropical fruits.

When Samuel returned with the tea pot, Ben asked, "There are only a few guests here this morning?"

"There are plenty, but businessmen go before seven to office, and tourists come down after eight."

"I see."

"Enjoy breakfast. You take anti-malarial, sir?"

"Yes, thank you. Breakfast is good." Samuel was uneducated, but he understood his guests and their needs. Ben resolved to talk more with him about the other guests.

After his breakfast he left a note at the front desk for Rosa, asking to see her that evening after offices closed at 5:30. He wanted to discuss details of the conference receptions and banquets. Then he returned to his room and collected his files for the conference. He packaged the white stones from Hudu in a dark plastic bag with some spare British change that he had declared at the airport, so the bag would jingle innocently. He filled his shoulder bag and returned to the hotel lobby. Shortly before nine o'clock Dean Gomez arrived in the university car with his driver. Ben climbed in the back and they sped off.

Gomez greeted him, "Good morning. I hope you are well today."

"Fine, but tired from the trip. Are you and your family well?"

"All well.

"I phoned for appointments. First we pay a courtesy call on the Minister of the Interior for permission to hold the conference. Next we go to Tourism to inspect the translation equipment. Then you will be my guest for lunch at the Faculty Club."

"Excellent. I hope everything goes well."

Ben could see the Ministry of the Interior with army tanks guarding the approach roads. The soldiers recognized the vehicle and waved it through a roadblock. Ben and Gomez got out of the car in front of the gate to an old colonial office building. It was a two-story brick building with long covered verandahs running around it to keep the sun from heating the walls. Policemen at the guardhouse phoned the Minister's office to confirm their appointment. Then one of them escorted Ben and Gomez inside. They crossed a garden and mounted Spanish steps outside the building to the second floor. Modern sliding glass doors led into the Minister's reception room, wood-paneled and excessively air-conditioned. His female secretary was stylishly dressed and wore straightened hair. She purred their names, "Dean Gomez and Dr. Mchunguzi. Please sit down and wait while the Minister is in conference."

"Thank you," replied Dean Gomez. "I presume he has a file prepared on the World Economics Conference that will begin on Wednesday?"

"Certainly," she answered curtly.

"Good," he replied and then looked at Ben. "While we wait we will discuss arrangements for this important international event bringing over one hundred world-renowned professionals to Miseria."

They sat down on some overstuffed sofas and reviewed several files together. The secretary read official documents while the police guard stood near the door. After twenty minutes she telephoned. A few minutes later a well-dressed man emerged from the door beside her desk.

"Dean Gomez, good to see you."

"May I present Dr. Mchunguzi, Regional Secretary of the World Economics Association, recently arrived from London."

"Happy to meet you, Your Excellency."

"Happy to meet you too, Doctor. Please come in. Salina, bring the files."

His office was large and luxurious. A huge desk sat in front of large windows that looked out on the government office district. On one wall was a huge map of the administrative regions of Miseria. On the other wall beneath a flattering color portrait of the President were pictures of the Minister meeting foreign dignitaries. From their chairs in front of the Minister's desk, Dean Gomez and Ben had difficulty distinguishing the Minister's facial features because of sunlight behind him.

The Minister paused to examine the files his secretary brought him. Then he looked up. "The conference begins on Wednesday?"

"Yes, but many important delegates will arrive tomorrow," answered Dean Gomez. "We plan for them to rest at the Grand Hotel, take a tour of the capital and the University, and shop before the conference opens officially. Will there be any difficulty receiving your letter authorizing the conference?"

The Minister thought a moment and then replied, "First, please check the list of delegates to make sure that there have been no changes."

Ben responded, "Two delegates from Europe and one each from Lesotho and Uganda have cancelled their plans to attend. I have prepared a revised list here to give you. In addition, we will cancel the contract for a European technician for translation equipment, if the Ministry of Tourism can supply us with a Miserian specialist."

"Very well. I am glad you are trying to employ local people rather than importing experts. Are any of your speakers paid for their work?"

"They were paid for papers that they sent to the World Economics Association but not for delivering them here in Miseria."

"I see. So there will be no problem with work permits from the Ministry of Labor."

"No problem at all," said Ben, hoping to sound confident.

"Are there any additions to the list of delegates?" the Minister continued.

"We ended enrollment for the conference three months ago, so that we could assure there were no surprise additions."

The Minister hesitated and then said gravely, "Very well. I have the letter of authorization. You may sign it, and then I will put the official seal on it."

"Thank you very much, Your Excellency," said Ben as he received the document.

Dean Gomez then asked, "Has there been any progress in finding the murderer of Professor Hudunu?"

"The investigation is continuing. I have put some good personnel on it," the Minister answered defensively.

"Who is in charge of the investigation?"

"I named Cristobal Mulama. He is our liaison to Interpol. If there are any international angles on the case, then he will be able to pursue them through the international police network."

"An intelligent man, and neutral with regard to the town of Hudu. Thank you for your choice, Your Excellency."

The three men rose and shook hands. The Minister waved Dean Gomez and Ben out the door. In the reception room several well-dressed people were waiting their turn to see the politician. Dean Gomez thanked the secretary and the policeman who escorted them back to the gate. His chauffeur brought the car, and they started for the Ministry of Tourism.

"Is Mulama a good choice for investigator?" asked Ben.

"His family is from the capital, so they are not part of the dispute between the towns of Hudu and Sodu. He is intelligent, so the government put him in his position with Interpol in order to investigate for fraud among foreign businessmen who operate here. The government Ministers want to be sure they will honor their contracts, both the written ones and the hidden ones. Mulama lives in a three-story villa in a fashionable neighborhood that he could not pay for on his government salary. Obviously he is worth more to the politicians than the bribes he takes."

Ben hesitated and then asked a question that troubled him, "So many Miserians live off of businesses. Do you have business income on the side too?"

"Only some royalties from my *History of Miseria* textbook. I had it published by a Miserian press. We had to offer half the royalties to the then Minister of Education, so it would be adopted officially. When he was jailed, his successor demanded a half-share of the contract too. I receive two thousand bars a year as my share."

"Does your family own property?"

"Yes. In fact, you can see it from your hotel room. We own part of the coconut plantation near the hotel. We once owned the land for the hotel and part of the business district, but the colonial government condemned it and gave it to European businesses."

"Did you contact the workers who live in the coconut plantation to discover if they know anything about Hudunu's murder?"

"They are members of my family! We had a meeting Saturday night before I came to see you at the hotel."

Ben chuckled. "You did not tell me that."

"I did not know you well. And you never asked me." Gomez became serious. "The police arrived Saturday afternoon. They took the young men to the beach and threatened to beat them if they did not confess. They led elders into their houses and threatened to humiliate them before the others if they did not talk. After many appeals and some bribes they left. I had to go to help calm them down and assure them I would intervene to protect them."

"Did they see anything?"

"No. They claim no one came from the east that evening. None of my family or the other families would have committed a murder like that either."

"I was not suggesting it."

"We would use other ways to punish our enemies."

The Ministry of Tourism was situated on the road to the airport in the diplomatic district. No security police were around it. A watchman met them at the gate. They crossed a courtyard where two old tourist buses were jacked up with their tires removed. The small building was nicely whitewashed, but lack of maintenance gave it a tired look. The sagging door they entered creaked and threatened to fall off. The office inside had old desks and chairs in it. Manual typewriters sat on desks. A wire dangled from the single light fixture in the center of the room to an electric calculator.

The secretary was wearing a colorful African dress and greeted them with a pleasant smile, "How are you, Dean Gomez? How is the University?"

"Very well, Lucia. And you?"

"Fine."

"May I introduce Dr. Mchunguzi from Kenya, who is responsible for the World Economics Association Conference this week."

"Happy to meet you. From Kenya? Not many Kenyans come to Miseria. Welcome!"

"Thank you. I find Miseria a friendly country."

Gomez stated their business. "We came to see about the translation equipment for the conference."

"I see. The chauffeur has the key to the storeroom. He took a French visitor to the Immigration Bureau to extend his visa."

"When do you expect them back?"

"They left before eight o'clock. They could come back soon or late depending on the Immigration people."

"Does the Director have the key?"

"He is not here yet."

"When do you expect him?"

"Maybe in an hour."

"Does he have the key?"

"Maybe so."

"Could we call him?"

"If the phone works!"

"Suppose we go to the Immigration Bureau and find the driver."

"You do not know the van."

"How can we identify it or the driver?"

"Don't worry. I will come with you."

She bustled about, putting away her papers and locking her desk. Then she carefully locked the office door and took the key out to the street, passed the watchman at the gate, and gave the key to a woman selling peanuts by the roadside. Lucia smiled and explained. "That woman will look after the building while I am away." She cheerily took the front seat of the car and gave the driver directions.

On the way Ben asked, "Why did you not give the key to the watchman?"

"I do not trust him."

"Why?"

"He comes from a family of thieves."

"Why did the Ministry hire him then?"

"If he has a job, the family will not bother the Ministry."

Ben smiled at her logic and then asked a question to check his understanding. "But if he will not rob the Ministry, why do you not leave the key with him?"

"If I leave the key, he will rob us so they will blame me."

"I see. Do you trust the peanut seller then?"

"Of course. She is the Director's niece. No one else has the right to sell in front of the Ministry of Tourism!"

At the Immigration Bureau they found the chauffeur and convinced him to entrust them with the key. On the way back

Ben asked her if the translation equipment worked. "Maybe so," she replied.

She opened her office again and led them down a hall. She opened a dark storage closet and pointed to a jumble of wires. "Here is the translation equipment."

Ben looked at Gomez. "Do you have a technician at the University who could repair this stuff?"

"I don't know if anyone could. I can see vacuum tubes back there." Turning to Lucia, he added, "Would you allow me to take this equipment to the University and ask the technician to service it?"

She looked doubtful, then replied, "Only if you sign an official receipt for it."

"I shall gladly sign it."

She went back to the front door and shouted to the watchman to call the university driver and come in to pick up the equipment. Then she returned to her desk and efficiently composed a receipt with two carbon copies for the equipment. Dean Gomez signed them while Ben supervised the men carrying out the mass of wires, amplifiers, speakers, and microphones. All the equipment was still plugged together, and they dared not unplug it for fear of never finding connections again. Ben also did not want any trailing wires to get stuck in the doorways. Dean Gomez walked out of the office just as the three men marched across the courtyard with their loads linked together by wires. "In Miseria intellectuals are never expected to carry heavy loads," he called smiling.

"In my country elders and important people do not do manual work either," Ben answered. "But I am emancipating myself!"

In the car Ben wet his handkerchief from his water flask to clean dust off himself. He asked Gomez to stop by the bank on the way to the University. They arrived there at 11:30 at the height of the rush to finish business before the noon closing. Ben was dismayed to see the long lines at the counter.

At the same time he was pleased that the bank was staffed entirely by Africans. Unperturbed by the crowd Dean Gomez walked through to the manager's office. He introduced Ben to his former student. While they exchanged small talk, an assistant cashed a thousand dollars in travelers checks for just over five thousand bars. Within ten minutes they were back in the car.

On the way to the University they passed the old colonial secondary boarding school. It had an imposing gate and circular drive through the remains of formal gardens and water fountains. Three stories tall with a massive flight of steps running up to the administrative offices on the second floor and huge classroom wings spread on both sides, it was designed to inspire awe in the privileged few Miserians who attended.

Today it looked much the worse for wear. Roof tiles were missing, and the whitewash had succumbed to mold. In the former gardens students lounged under the surviving trees. Market women crowded outside the rusty iron-grill fence to sell them snacks.

Ben asked Gomez, "Did the Ministry of Education stop the school's maintenance budget?"

"No, the Ministry created secondary schools in the main towns, because the purpose of this school was to separate young Miserians from the ancestral culture and force them to adopt European culture. The school would draw them near the seat of power. Logically they should have closed the dormitories and converted them to more classrooms. At the same time the staff of the Ministry were graduates of this, the only secondary school under colonialism. So they kept it as a boarding school, without sufficient budget for the students' room and board. That is why those women sell the students so many snacks, to supplement the starchy food in the refectory. It is an example of poor planning by the Ministry."

At the university gate Dean Gomez ordered one of the

watchmen into the car to help them with the load in the trunk. They arrived at the science building, where the janitor also helped unload the car. Inside they found the electrical engineering professor in a laboratory dismissing a class of students. Dean Gomez introduced him to Ben and asked him to call a lab technician about repairing the translation equipment.

A smiling young man named Antonio soon appeared. After exchanging greetings, Dean Gomez told him to inspect the equipment by four o'clock to see if it could be made to work. He could buy any spare parts he needed and hire any help he wished. If it worked, he would get a bonus of a week's wages and another week's bonus for serving as technician during the conference. To show the funds available Gomez asked Ben to advance the engineering professor one thousand bars for purchases, provided the receipts were proper. Eyes lit up at the sight of the money. Ben was impressed. Clearly they would give it their best try. The engineering professor spoke eloquently for the benefit of the students about the important contribution they could make to the international conference, not just making money.

As they left, Ben explained to Gomez about the white pellets he had bought in the market and asked if the chemistry department could analyze them. They found a young professor in his office and told him about the sample, including Ben's suspicions. The chemistry professor was also eager to show his ability to the visiting dignitary and promised to examine them that evening. Ben mentioned the precautions he had taken lest the rocks were toxic, so the professor would not contaminate himself.

Well satisfied, they drove to the administration building. Dean Gomez dismissed his driver for lunch and told him to return to the Faculty Club at 1:30. At his office, he introduced Ben to his secretary, a young man named Hector. Ben chatted while Dean Gomez checked his messages, made some calls, and signed some authorizations. He also scheduled afternoon appointments with the two students and an employee who had been waiting for him to return. When they left, Hector complained that he had offered to make their appointments, but that they expected to wait so they could see the big man themselves. Gomez tried calling Immigration at the airport about Ben's passport, but all lines out of the campus were busy. "Don't worry," he assured Ben. "We will get through eventually." They washed up in a faculty restroom that was pleasantly clean.

They had a peaceful walk to the Faculty Club. The university buildings had been designed with concrete coverings along the sides to protect pedestrians from sun and rain. Open areas between buildings were shaded by flame of the forest trees with their bright red and green color and neem trees with their insecticide properties. Students who passed made friendly greetings to the Dean.

"I enjoy this campus," said Ben.

"So do I," answered Gomez. "But last year before our first planning meeting for the conference it was tense here. The students wanted to strike over political issues. I could not allow it, even though I agreed with them. Some hard-line Cabinet Ministers wanted a student strike so they could send in soldiers to quash it as an example to the rest of the population."

"They do not respect academic freedom."

"They do not understand freedom, only power."

"How did you deal with the strike?"

"Fortunately, the Spanish government had given twenty scholarships for graduate study. I contacted some key students and gave them a choice of confronting the government or going to Europe. Most of them preferred to leave, and the others felt sold out."

"Did you create an incentive for other student leaders to organize a strike later?"

"Perhaps next year. But this year your conference and Hudunu's murder are keeping them preoccupied."

They left the bright outdoors for the calm half-light of the Faculty Club. Inside there was a parlor with cool rattan chairs and newspapers. As they entered everyone stood. Dean Gomez introduced Ben: "Here is our guest of honor, Dr. Benjamin Mchunguzi Maluum from the World Economics Association." He greeted Bongo, the Assistant Minister of the Commission on Higher Education and member of the conference planning committee, whose eyes shifted nervously in the company of academics. He also met the Chancellor of the University, a distinguished gray-haired gentleman. He also recognized Señora Gomez, the Dean's wife. Dossou and Zande were smiling as they shook his hand. They introduced their economist colleague, Professor Stepan, an austere figure with a dignified handshake and tinted glasses. Ben addressed him, "I have heard so much about you that I am happy to meet you finally."

"It is an honor for me too," he replied in a German accent.

"May I invite you to dine," said Dean Gomez as he ushered them toward a long table reserved for their party. He seated his wife at the end of the table with Ben on her right and the Chancellor on her left. Bongo sat next to Ben and Stepan across from Bongo. Zande and Dossou were at the other end with the host. The restaurant manager brought white wine and filled their glasses. Gomez proposed a toast to the success of the World Economics Conference.

Ben had not expected a formal European dinner and would have preferred to sit with his friends at the other end of the table. Señora Gomez was an accomplished dinner hostess and quickly started a conversation about Ben's family and how they adapted to life in London. She then drew out the Chancellor, who told about his culture shock going from Miseria to a university in Spain. She told stories about accompanying her husband on an official tour of Chinese universities. "Oh la la, they eat everything in China," she exclaimed. Ben looked at the first course of pink boiled shrimp surrounding white mayonnaise sauce with a colorful border of sliced raw carrots, cucumbers, and papaya. He wondered if the Faculty Club had been challenged to outdo the Chinese.

He asked Bongo about his travels, but the nervous Commissioner was not in a story-telling mood. So he wondered, "Are there Miserian graduates studying business administration in order to manage large modern enterprises?"

"We have some studying in the United States and Europe. We have not had any return to take over businesses yet," Bongo replied defensively.

When the next course arrived, Gomez announced triumphantly, "We ordered a Miserian specialty, chicken in blood stew." The waiters served them rice topped with chicken in a thick dark sauce, cooked greens, and broiled pineapple slices.

Upon tasting it, Ben told his host, "This sauce is excellent."

"Yes, Europeans do not cook meat in its blood, even though it is an excellent source of nutrition. There is an obscure verse in Leviticus that forbids such practices among the Hebrew people. No matter how atheist they have become, Europeans still follow that verse in their food habits."

Ben sensed a conversation opening with Stepan. "Do you agree with the Dean's assessment of European food habits?"

"I am not an atheist, but my people traditionally made blood sausage."

"Which Miserian dishes have you come to appreciate?"

"I like this dish, the superb ocean fish, french fried vegetables, palm hearts, and I cannot eat enough tropical fruits," he explained methodically.

"Have you lived in other parts of Africa?"

"I worked on a United Nations mission in Congo-Brazzaville."

"How did you like it there?"

"I prefer Miseria. It is more peaceful here, and I like the University."

"You are welcome here," interjected Dean Gomez.

"Thank you. For a refugee, like myself, your hospitality is very important."

Dossou asked, "With the political changes in Eastern Europe, are you still a refugee?"

"I have been a refugee for forty years. I do not know where my relatives and friends are back there."

"Can you telephone these days to try to locate them?"

"I don't know." He added dejectedly, "It would be expensive."

Señora Gomez continued sympathetically, "We all recognize how important family is to everyone. We hope that you can find them and then return to your home here."

"Thank you, Madam. You are most gracious."

Dossou was warming up. "I heard a story about the South African president, who tried to phone his dead predecessor in hell. He did not want any official record of the call, so he told the operator it was a private matter to put on his home phone bill and he did not want to talk more than five minutes. He reached his predecessor, and they started talking about problems with apartheid, rowdy politicians, ungrateful Black people."

They all chuckled.

"And he noticed the call had lasted twenty minutes. So he finished the conversation and then called the operator to complain that the call was not supposed to cost him so much. 'Don't worry,' answered the operator, 'Hell is a local call here.' " His belly shook as he laughed.

"I guess militarized societies provoke that kind of humor," suggested Zande. "In Egypt I heard that President Nasser died and went to the Egyptian hell. The Devil decided to show off, so he sent him to the rack, but it had broken down for lack of foreign spare parts." Bongo shifted in his seat. "Then he sent him to the lake of fire, but they had a shortage of kerosene so it was turned off. Finally the Devil sent him back to live in Egypt, because he decided it was the worst punishment to give him."

As if on cue a flaming dessert arrived. A waiter brought bananas in a frying pan, poured on sauce and liqueur, and lit them. It was a delicious spectacle. "Bananas flambé, the specialty of the Faculty Club," Gomez announced proudly. "The club makes its own chocolate rum for these. And it pays taxes on the rum," he added, looking at Bongo.

"I am impressed," responded Ben. "British cooking seldom produces such surprises."

"Does your wife cook Kenyan dishes in London?" asked Señora Gomez.

"Yes, but we cannot get good African ingredients. The only bananas we can find have sat in the hold of a ship for months. Other spices we have to wait for friends to bring."

The others nodded in sympathy.

The waiters gave them a choice of espresso coffee or tea.

"Where do the coffee and tea come from?" asked Ben out of habit.

"Coffee from Ivory Coast and tea from Kenya," replied the waiter.

Ben smiled, "I must have tea then."

When they finished, Ben asked the question that had been troubling him. "Now that Hudunu has passed on, we no longer have a chairperson for the local arrangements committee. Since the other members of the committee are here, would one of you be willing to take over?" He looked at Dean Gomez, who had averted his eyes. Then he looked at Bongo, who eyes suddenly began to gleam. He said hesitantly, "Commissioner Bongo, would you be willing to meet this evening with Rosa and me in order to work out the details?"

Bongo's eyes became intense. "We must meet another

time. I have an important reception this evening at the Presidential Palace."

Ben tried to sound sincere. "I am sorry. Hudunu and I had planned to meet with her on Saturday. Tomorrow the conference delegates begin to arrive. We cannot delay further." Bongo's eyes went blank again, and Ben felt relieved. The negotiations would be difficult enough without Bongo along.

He looked over at Dossou. "Professor Dossou, would you come this evening to meet her?"

Dossou smiled apologetically. "Much as I would enjoy her company, I have to finish my work at the University in order to be ready on Wednesday for the conference." He looked at Gomez for approval.

Zande shook his head as well. Stepan showed no interest.

Ben looked at Gomez as well. "I have already taken much of your time. However, could you help with this meeting as well?" He turned to Señora Gomez. "With your permission, Madam?" Her look told him his quest was futile.

Gomez answered, "I believe we all have confidence in your negotiations with Rosa. We have already discussed with her the hospitality we expect. All that remain are the details of payment, which you are responsible for."

Ben felt he was being put on the spot. In Miseria they set high standards for hospitality; now he would have to finance lavish entertainment. "She is a very shrewd businesswoman who knows that without Hudunu our plans are in disarray. Will she not take advantage of us?"

Gomez continued authoritatively, "As a Miserian she respects Hudunu's memory. She also knows that her good reputation depends on us."

Ben winced. If the entertainment was on a scale necessary to honor Professor Hudunu's memory in Miserian fashion, he would go bankrupt.

Gomez changed his tune. "Remember, she was married to a German businessman for twenty years, so she can also understand your budget limitations too. If there are any problems, you could phone the rest of us, and we will talk to her."

"Thank you. The Board of Directors of the World Economics Association does have strict budget standards, which we cannot exceed. I will do my best and call you if necessary."

They all rose, shook hands, and said goodbyes.

The university driver was at the door to take Dean and Señora Gomez home and Ben to his hotel. Ben made sure Señora Gomez knew she was invited to the opening reception of the conference.

Returning to the hotel, he was surprised to find De Almeida's son waiting for him in the lobby. He greeted him warmly and was pleased to receive his passport with a visa freshly stamped. To thank him, Ben treated him to a sandwich at the hotel grill and then saw him off on his motorbike. At the front desk, he picked up a message from Rosa confirming their meeting that evening. He went up to his room and took a long-awaited siesta.

The telephone rang shortly after four. It was the engineering professor, who reported, "Good news. Antonio has both amplifiers working, as well as four microphones. He has tested sixty headphones that work on all four channels. Ten have problems with some channels. He has thirty more to test. I would estimate that we have over eighty fully functioning earphone sets."

"Congratulations! Tell Antonio and his helpers that they earned their bonus."

"We used some vacuum tubes from other equipment that cost 385 bars when we ordered them, and we need some spares and replacement wire to maintain the system for the conference."

"How much will it all cost?"

"Almost one thousand bars."

Ben had expected that answer. "I will authorize it. Give

me official receipts. Will the spares be useful for your lab afterward?"

"Yes, they will. We have some old instruments. Thank you."

"How many people helped Antonio?"

"He sent for an electronics worker from a business in the capital, who came during his lunch and siesta break. Also three of my students stayed to help test ear phones."

"And you too?"

"I stayed to supervise."

"Thank you, I will be sure to tell Dean Gomez how helpful the engineering department has been."

"We were glad to be of service."

"Goodbye."

He called Lucia immediately. After several tries the switchboard completed the call. "Lucia, this is Dr. Mchunguzi from Kenya."

"Doctor, how are you?"

"Very well. I have good news: The translation equipment is working well."

"Fine."

"Does the Minister agree to let us use it for the conference?"

"Fine. I showed him the receipt from Dean Gomez and he said, 'Fine.' "

"Very good. The university engineers put new vacuum tubes in it and new wiring, so it will be improved when we return it to the Ministry."

"Fine."

"Did the Minister receive his invitation to the opening reception of the conference?"

"Yes, he is coming."

"Very well. Goodbye."

Ben called the Minister of the Interior and left word with the secretary that they would not require a European translation technician. He then decided to see what the commercial district looked like. Leaving the hotel he was assailed by taxi drivers, convinced that he could not walk a block on his own. He persevered in his refusal and they soon left him when a party of American tourists appeared from the lobby.

The sleepy business district had small shops open to the street. Their steel shutters were rolled back, and Miserian salespeople stood guard over the goods on open tables. The proprietor sat at the back next to the cash register. The proprietor's name was listed above the door, "Traficant Brothers," or "Cartagena and Son." The shop with "Lugner and Company" etched in the cement wall now had a wooden sign saying, "Independence Store." Its proprietor was Miserian. Ben casually walked in and priced Chinese flashlight batteries and talcum powder. Prices were 20 percent higher than they had been six months earlier. He also looked at imported brocades, which were better quality than the cottons he bought in Hudu. He bargained half-heartedly with the proprietor to see how expensive these goods were and realized that in local currency they were out of reach. If he exchanged his foreign currency on the parallel market where it was worth 50 percent more, he would have enough bars to buy brocade cheaply.

Instead, he went across to the main post office. Again, it was an old colonial building with a flight of stairs in front. He had to pass several leprous beggars to get inside. He greeted the employee and bought some beautiful stamps in red, yellow, and green, Miseria's national colors. He wanted to let his family and colleagues in London know that he had arrived safely, and his parents in Kenya that the conference was beginning. He mentioned that his friend Hudunu had died, but did not go into details for fear of censorship. On the way out, he handed his small change to the eldest beggar and informed the group they should divide it fairly. He was pleased to see that in traditional fashion the others calmly awaited the elder's decision about their portion of the gift.

Returning to the hotel, he showered and shaved in preparation for his meeting with Rosa. At 5:30 he descended to her office. Her door stated "Señora Rosa Lugner" in memory of her deceased German husband, the successful businessman who had owned Lugner and Company. She wore a shimmering pink brocade dress with large eyelets that revealed her smooth, dark skin. Expensive perfume wafted through the air.

"You look lovely this evening," he said sincerely.

"Thank you. I want you to feel welcome in Miseria," she replied coquettishly.

"I do, after the initial shock on Saturday."

"I miss Hudunu too. But the conference must go on! Can I get you a drink?"

"Something light."

"Dubonnet, sherry, or a mixed drink?"

"Sherry, please."

"Which kind?"

"Whichever you recommend."

She proceeded to pour old Spanish sherry the European way into two glasses without the Miserian ceremony of transferring the drink from one to another before testing it.

He looked around her office. He could not tell if she had prepared it for work or seduction. On one side her mahogany desk had files arranged neatly upon it. On the other side, a table was set for two. Each place setting had forks for appetizer, entree, and dessert along with goblets for wine, water, and champagne.

She handed him his glass and then led him to the chair beside her desk. She raised her glass, "To the success of your conference."

"And to your health, Señora."

They sipped their sherry in silence for a moment.

"Did you know Hudunu well?" Ben asked.

"Not very well. I knew him from parties and then from the negotiations for this conference. He is not related to me. Still, I was shocked by his murder. Did you know him well?"

"We met each other in university in the United States and at economics conferences like this one. I counted him a good friend and colleague. Was he at the hotel Friday evening?"

She looked irritated. "He must have come . . . to go swimming like that. He did not come to see me, though."

"I was not suggesting that," Ben said soothingly. "I just thought you would know the hotel employees and what they were saying."

"I asked them. They said he came and then he left."

"Whom do you think killed him?"

"I suspect it was political. Professor Hudunu did not hide his opinions about the government."

"What did he say about the government."

She answered softly as if to avoid eavesdroppers. "He called it a 'kleptocracy.' "

"Is it really 'government by thieves'?"

"Only if you believe it is unethical to help your family members when you have the power to do so."

"Hudunu helped his family. He was remembered for it at his funeral."

"Yes, if politicians are remembered for giving gifts at family funerals and town celebrations, people will forget that the money was not theirs to give away."

"So under a system of clientelism, it is the followers who are at fault, not just the leaders."

"Gift giving is built into Miserian family structure. Is it not so in Kenya too?"

"I am afraid it is."

"Are Kenyan intellectuals not in trouble when they say it is unethical?"

"They are liable to be fired or arrested."

Again she spoke softly. "Miseria is not a democracy, unlike

Kenya. We cannot rely on legal protection if we oppose the politicians."

"So we cannot expect the murderer to be found and punished?"

She answered grimly, "No. Do not expect justice."

"Well, what do we need to discuss about the entertainment plans?"

She picked up one of her files. "Have you seen the plans and the contract?"

"Yes, I have copies of them. And I approved them, as I stated in my letter to you."

"Good. I told Professor Hudunu that we would have to adjust the costs in case of inflation."

"I am sure you knew six months ago that inflation was inevitable. You should have included expected inflation in your estimates."

"Inflation has risen 25 percent in six months. Before it was only 20 percent per year. So we need to raise our prices by 15 percent."

Ben winced. For these negotiations he had wanted reinforcement from the local arrangements committee. "I agree that Miserian prices have risen 10 to 15 percent faster than before. And I am willing to adjust the bill that much to pay waiters and hotel costs. However, most of the cost of entertainment is for imported goods. These rise in price at the same rate as in Europe, which is to say, only about 5 percent per year."

"The reason for the rise in Miserian prices is that government import duties have risen suddenly. As a condition for making new loans to Miseria, the International Monetary Fund imposed a structural adjustment program, which requires the government to cut budget and trade deficits. It raised taxes on luxury imports and cut subsidies for grain and sugar, which caused prices to rise in general."

Ben spoke softly this time. "I thought that many of the

brands of alcohol and canned goods that we will consume must be paid for in foreign currency because they are smuggled in. So Miserian import taxes do not apply to them anyway."

Rosa looked vexed and whispered back. "Everyone is trying to cope with inflation by raising incomes. The Customs inspectors who let through the contraband demand 25 percent higher bribes now."

"We have ordered a reception booth in Immigration and transport to the hotel, bus tours of the city on Tuesday and Wednesday, a reception and dance for two hundred people Wednesday evening, organizer breakfasts each morning — though that is not an African tradition! — hospitality for the two villages we visit on Friday, a visit to the lagoon on Sunday afternoon, and a closing banquet for one hundred on Tuesday plus service and gratuities. For this I brought bank drafts made out in bars to the hotel and dollars for the imports."

He made his power play by putting the two checks from his carrying case on her desk. She looked at them impassively. He pulled out a plastic bag with twenty one-hundred-dollar bills in it, which he hoped did not smell like his jogging shoes. She counted them mechanically, snapping each one like a bank teller. Then he pulled out an envelope with eight one-hundred-dollar bills and said. "I planned to give eight hundred dollars for incidentals and tips."

Her eyes flickered with interest. "Make it one thousand dollars and I accept the deal."

Ben tried again, "I have a conference budget to meet. Would one hundred more be sufficient? Otherwise, we could drop the breakfasts."

"You pay in bars for breakfast. We would have to drop the gift to the Chiefs of the villages," she countered shrewdly.

"No, the villages are showing us hospitality; we must return the favor in kind. Could you serve palm wine at the receptions?"

"Never! These are the elite of Miseria. I would never serve them beverages from the bush!" She sat rigidly, her eyes flashing.

Ben sank in his chair. "Well, my budget now is exceeded. I have to use my own funds. Will you take one hundred and fifty?"

"Inflation hurts me too. One hundred and eighty."

"One hundred and sixty?"

"One hundred and seventy."

He pulled out his wallet, removed three fifties and one twenty, and handed them to her. He smiled at her. "This truly is my own money."

She glanced at him. "I know. But I want to cover my costs."

"Would you please sign a receipt for the bank drafts and an informal one for the currency."

"You realize it is not legal in Miseria for me to sign for the currency."

"I will not use it here. I must justify my expenditures to the accountants in London."

She sighed, "All right, I trust you," signed the receipt, and slipped the money into her drawer.

He sipped his sherry and looked at her admiringly. "If the IMF had negotiated with you, Miseria would be better off today."

She relaxed. "We women are not allowed to run the politics, which is why we run the Miserian economy."

"Why is it that foreign businesses still thrive in the commercial district then?"

"My husband owned one of them."

"Today is it called 'Independence Store'?"

"I renamed it after independence, because my husband transferred ownership to me to avoid any nationalization of foreign-owned property. He kept his interest in this hotel, thinking the government would not dare interfere in the tourist business."

"But you compete with Traficant, a Frenchman, and Cartagena, a Spaniard?"

"Cartagena is dead. His successors are incompetent, so I do not worry about them. I have an arrangement with Traficant. I vote his shares in the hotel; he helps me run the store. We don't compete," she said smugly.

"So the hotel was nationalized after all?"

"Yes, the European director refused to negotiate sale of stock to some politicians, so they decreed it had to be majority-owned by Miserians. My husband and Traficant saw it coming and transferred their stock to my name. Now I own 55 percent of the hotel. The other foreign owners were bought out for a pittance."

"By you?"

"No. By the politicians. I would have offered more than they did, but once I had control I wanted political protection."

"Clever woman. Which politicians?"

"The Ministers of Tourism and Finance. They have changed since, but their successors take on ownership."

"Did you object to them becoming business partners?"

"No, they help provide business and facilitate currency transactions."

"Do they have the same arrangements with the American hotel?"

"No, it is set up under an international convention negotiated between the hotel chain and the government. That way they obtained maximum concessions from the government. The hotel is protected from political harassment, because a dispute is decided by an outside arbitrator, not through the Miserian legal system. Their real protection, though, is their international reservation system and business arrangements with airlines and tour companies. If a politician tried to interfere too much, the company could shut off the flow of guests."

"Do you resent their privileged competition the way your hotel director, Musa, seems to?"

"No. They do take some tourist business away, but their presence enables me to show my politician partners that this hotel must benefit from the same advantages. I believe we are better off because they are here."

"Could you have opposed their coming?"

"Perhaps. It is easy to prevent development. But I did not try to."

"You are a shrewd woman!"

"I learned business from my husband."

"So our conference will benefit your hotel as well as your catering service," Ben concluded.

"Yes, it will. Do you realize I gave you a good deal on the catering? We could not raise room rates, because they were published, so we have to absorb the cost increases. We wanted to cover our costs on the catering."

"I understand. Will you make a profit on the rooms too?"

"Of course, most of our costs are sunk in the building. So higher capacity is always profitable, but inflation raises the replacement or expansion costs. Still, we have had to raise current expense for our staff's wages in response to inflation, since they are barely able to live as it is."

"Could you afford to raise their wages above subsistence?"

"That is no solution. Since there are plenty of people willing to work for subsistence wages, we do not need to raise them. If we did so, more family members would arrive from the villages to live off our workers' wages. Higher wages just create more urban unemployment."

"Yes, this is what an economist named Todaro said. In Kenya we had an agreement between business, labor unions, and the government to raise employment in the late 1960s.

However, the announcement of the agreement just caused more people to flock to the cities looking for jobs. Unemployment is not an easy problem to solve."

"We don't want more urban unemployment, because it leads to social unrest."

"Do your relatives live off your income too?"

"No, I learned to live without my relatives. They abandoned me when I married Lugner instead of continuing my studies. They wanted me to go to university, get a job in the civil service, and share my income with them. Now that I have more income than a civil servant, I remind them that they cursed me before."

"Whom did they want you to marry?"

"An old politician with other wives already."

"So you married for love?"

"Yes. Lugner was a good man and took me seriously." She gave him a misty look. "Do you take your wife seriously, Dr. Mchunguzi?"

"Yes!" He looked at her in surprise, not knowing what her question was about. "I married for love too. She is a university graduate. If I did not take her seriously, she would let me know."

"Good. That is the way it should be. Shall we move to the table for dinner." She picked up the phone and rang the kitchen for service.

They moved to the exquisitely set table where she lit candles and dimmed the indirect lighting. Their meal proceeded through multiple courses: baked fish in wine sauce, imported filet mignon, lettuce with vinaigrette, assorted cheeses, flan in rum, espresso and liqueur. Ben complimented her sincerely on each perfect course, but the cumulative effect became unpleasant.

As the meal began he had felt a close rapport with Rosa, but by the end he suspected that she had stage-managed their frank conversation to achieve some effect. As they sipped their espresso he asked her, "Why did you tell me about your ownership of the hotel? I did not need to know in order to do business with you."

"I told you so that you would trust that your foreign exchange is safe with me. I will respect our contract like any European businessman, even though the contract is not legally enforceable."

He did not want to appear weak. "I know that. But we both know your reputation is important to receive repeat business."

"Yes, we both understand that. But we are both Africans, and we prefer to do business on the basis of personal ties." She smiled. "I confided in you because you are a good friend, Dr. Mchunguzi."

"And our conference came here because you are a good friend, Señora Lugner." He smiled back.

"Shall we join the dance on the patio? It may be your last chance to enjoy yourself until the conference is over," she said lightly.

Ben excused himself to go to his room before meeting Rosa at the dance. He noticed the time was already past 9:30. The dinner had lasted a long time. Rosa's behavior still perplexed him. She had plenty of work to prepare for the conference, just as he did. Why was she entertaining him? She would not want for male companionship. Her income, connections, and good looks would provide plenty of admirers. He returned to the dance wondering about her.

She was talking to the bartender while waiting for him. Without a word, she took his hand and led him to the dance floor; her eyes pinned him with a long, sensuous scrutiny. She danced exquisitely without drawing attention to herself. Her body followed the rhythm of the band and his own movements.

He could not help comparing her to Teresa the night before. Teresa and he shared an enjoyable time together without any thought of using each other. With Rosa he was aware he was being manipulated, yet not sure how.

Still, he accepted the rhythms of the Afro-Cuban music by the excellent hotel band. Eventually a breeze came up from the ocean and his back chilled. He wondered if it were Hudunu's memory or the onset of malaria. He excused himself, said goodnight to Rosa, and returned to his room.

He took an extra anti-malarial tablet and some aspirin in case a fever came up. In his suspicion he carefully inspected his room and files to verify whether they had been searched during his absence. He was relieved to find that they were undisturbed, and the dust of talcum powder on the floor had only his footprints in it. Wrapped warmly in his covers he sought sleep, which in his exhausted state came quickly.

Chapter IV

Life in the Boiler Room

⊗

BEN AWOKE ABRUPTLY. His day's responsibilities crashed into his consciousness. He had not reviewed the registration packets, checked the staff scheduling, or even read most of the conference papers. He sat up and wrote a list of details to check, knowing that the arrival of delegates would interrupt his efforts to finish these duties.

Ben's body felt good again, and that was a relief. He slipped into his running gear, trotted downstairs, and slid out the side door to avoid any early arrivals in the lobby. Ben noticed that the watchman spotted him exiting, so he greeted him, "Good morning. Did you have a quiet night?"

"Yes, sir. A quiet night, thanks be to God. And you?"

"I awakened well. You are a good watchman when you see me leave the door." The man smiled. Ben continued, "Did you work on Friday night?"

"Yes, sir." He looked tearful. "It was terrible the Professor died."

"Did the police question you?"

"Yes, sir. They come at home and take me from my family." He was in tears.

"Did they beat you?"

97

"They keep me with no water or food and ask questions."

"When did they let you go?"

"After Saturday night."

"Was Professor Hudunu at the hotel Friday night?"

"He not come from hotel Friday night."

"How did he go to the beach."

"He come from beach."

"Did Professor Hudunu swim at the hotel?" Ben could not remember him ever swimming.

"No, sir. He not swim."

"Did he wear swimming trunks at the hotel?"

"No, sir. Tourist leave swimsuit. Front desk have swimsuit."

"Did the police ask you if the front desk had a swimsuit?"

"No, sir."

"Did the hotel pay you for working Saturday night?"

"I no work on Saturday night."

"If police did not take you, do you work Saturday night?"

"Yes, sir." Ben looked at the hotel to see if any one was watching their conversation, but the sunlight on the windows prevented him from seeing in.

"Does the hotel pay you if police take you?"

"I don't know, sir." He looked miserable.

Ben handed him a five-bar note. "You are a good watchman. Professor Hudunu was my friend."

The man smiled and answered, "Thank you, sir."

Ben trotted down the beach toward the palm plantations. He observed the deserted sand dune where Hudunu died. From it one could see the windows to the dining hall, but the room windows were obscured by palms in the garden. If the dining hall were closed, no witnesses would be likely to see the murder.

The coconut palms stood in rows along the beach. He could see through the plantation diagonally and at right angles. Still, there was enough underbrush there so that an assailant could hide even in daylight. He was relieved to see some children staring out at this weird figure running in the early morning. He waved at them. Ahead some fishermen repaired a canoe and mended nets. They greeted him politely as he jogged by them.

Even after a mile the coast continued with palm trees and no sign of a break. Signs marked the edges of plantations, though none of them said "property of the Gomez family." He spotted paths meandering into the coconut grove toward the workers' huts.

Ben turned and headed back toward the sun. He passed the fishermen again. This time the children ignored him as they observed gravely a European couple skinny-dipping at a discreet distance from the hotel. "For those children, adult nakedness is a sign of insanity. Only bewitched people appear without covering their loins," he mused as he ran past them.

He waved to the watchman as he turned back into the gate to the hotel. Arriving at his room, he found a note that Professors Curmudgeon and Pedant had arrived at five o'clock and were recuperating in their rooms. He showered and slipped into a safari suit to stay cool despite the day's exertions.

At breakfast, Samuel directed him to his customary table. "Good morning, sir. Did you awaken well?"

"I did. And you?"

"Very well, sir. Continental today?"

"Yes, the same." Ben selected his toast and fruit, while Samuel brought the tea. "Did you see me go running this morning?"

"Yes, sir."

"I passed the sand dune where the Professor died."

"I saw, sir."

"What time did the dining room close on Friday night?"

"At ten o'clock."

"What time did the waiters leave?"

"At ten-thirty." Samuel looked troubled.

"Did the waiters see anything before they left?"

"Oh no, sir!" Samuel left to greet another diner.

Ben finished his breakfast and signaled for more tea. When Samuel brought it, he continued, "When Professor Hudunu wore a swimsuit, was it from his house?"

Samuel was silent.

"Were lost swimsuits at the hotel front desk?"

Samuel nodded, looking ill.

"I will not tell the police. Do not tell anyone about my questions."

"Yes, sir," Samuel answered reflectively.

As Ben left the dining room, intending to return to his room and review attendance lists and registration packets, he tried to recall the faces of all the conferees so that he could welcome them in a familiar way.

The front desk clerk interrupted his thoughts with an urgent message. The airport welcome agent reported that two Americans had been taken into custody by the police. They had flown in for the conference in a private plane without flight clearance. Each aviation authority from Morocco to Miseria was protesting their violation of national airspace. They had been arrested on arrival. Ben could see problems arriving in a most unexpected manner.

He looked up their names on his arrival list. They were partners in a lucrative economic consulting firm from Southern California. Ben's list indicated they were expected that evening by commercial airliner.

He called Musa and explained the problem. The hotel manager gave him the name of the house lawyer, Ahmad Boma, who was politically well-connected. Ben called the lawyer, who offered to help if paid in foreign exchange. Ben accepted, knowing the Californians could easily cover the legal expenses.

Shortly after, Boma arrived in a chauffeur-driven Mercedes. He was a large rotund man with a big smile. He greeted Ben familiarly even though they had never met before.

"Dr. Mchunguzi," he called in a booming voice after the driver opened the door for him, "I am happy to meet you."

"Now to the airport," he instructed the driver.

"I am happy that you could help us," replied Ben, and he sat down. They shook hands. "The hotel recommended you very highly."

"I do what I can for them," he answered genially. "There are always legal problems."

"Is the hotel in trouble?"

"Not at all! But suppliers fail. Employees are sacked. Guests get in trouble with their bills. New partners arrive. Lawyers are needed throughout the hotel business!"

"Have you been called about the murder of Professor Hudunu?" asked Ben, remembering that police had searched the hotel and questioned the employees.

Boma's attitude became serious, "No, at the moment it is a police matter. Of course, once a suspect is arrested or if the hotel is somehow involved, my services may be required."

"I see," said Ben. "Do you have contacts in the police to indicate how the investigations are proceeding?"

"Last night at the Presidential Palace I talked to the Minister of the Interior, who said that he has followed the investigation closely and expects shortly a solution to the case."

"Let's hope so! How is the import-export business?" asked Ben as they left the commercial district.

"Depressed! We are an underdeveloped country. Where are you from Dr. Mchunguzi?"

"Kenya."

"Yes, Nairobi. A commercial and industrial center! Here we have no industry to speak of."

"If you had more industry and consumer goods could be

manufactured locally, would there be fewer business opportunities for importers?"

"No, the Miserian import-export firms would be better off. We would import machinery and parts. We could export some of our products if we were competitive in price and quality."

"Neighboring countries have tariffs against manufactured goods just as Miseria does."

"If we had some manufactured exports, our lawyers would negotiate treaties with other countries for reciprocal trade."

"So you would be better off?"

"Miseria would be better off!"

They were on the airport highway now. The Mercedes sped along, swerving nimbly around the potholes. It plowed through the crowds at bus stops. It zipped past roadblocks as soldiers saluted.

Ben asked, "What is the procedure for private plane flights in Africa?"

"Aviation law is the same everywhere. Countries have sovereignty over their airspace. They control landings and takeoffs within their national boundaries. They also determine the right to board or disembark passengers. Normally before the flight the pilot must file a flight plan. The national aviation authority contacts control towers along the route, which give automatic permission for overflights according to a system supervised by a United Nations agency. Before takeoff the pilot obtains air route clearance from the control tower that indicates the flight route has been cleared."

"Does the system ever fail?"

"Of course. Sometimes the national authorities do not receive complete notification or do not identify the plane correctly. Recently a pilot was shot down in North Africa by the air force. He had obtained air route clearance, but the tanker he flew was a modified military plane. The air force could not recognize it."

"Did he survive?"

"Yes. They were not trying to kill him, only stop him. He lost the plane, though."

"Who was responsible?"

"Eventually the country accepted responsibility, because the air force did not receive notification that the plane had been converted from the military version."

"So do you think this case of the Americans will be easy to handle?"

"The law is clear. But we must establish the facts before we enter a plea. I still do not know why anyone would want to fly ten thousand miles from California in a small plane. These men must be peculiar."

At the airport Boma and Ben strode to the detention center. Unlike the Immigration office, where Ben had spent exasperating hours on arrival, this space had a jail cell. Ben felt grateful that the lawyer accompanied him.

The Americans jumped to their feet when the newcomers entered. Boma ignored them and introduced Ben to Cristobal Mulama, Miseria's liaison to Interpol and Chief Inspector in the Hudunu murder case. Mulama shook his hand briefly, looking at him through half-closed eyelids. Ben explained, "The two Americans detained here are delegates to the World Economics Conference that begins tomorrow."

From the cell came a triumphant "Hear, Hear!"

Embarrassed, Ben continued, "They were scheduled to arrive on a commercial flight this evening." The cell was quiet now.

Mulama replied coldly "Well, they arrived in a private plane after violating the airspace of five African nations."

"I regret their mistake and ask that you treat them leniently." Ben hoped to break Mulama's icy attitude.

"May we see the prisoners?" interjected Boma authoritatively.

"Are you representing them?" asked Mulama.

"Yes, the World Economics Association retained me on their behalf," stated Boma.

"Come with me," said Mulama, who only took three steps to the jail door. "Here they are." He pointed through the door. Two corpulent, unshaven white men looked defiantly at them.

"Does the plane belong to them?" asked Boma to Mulama.

"Yes," the men stated in unison.

"We radioed American authorities and confirmed it was registered in their names," Mulama stated, ignoring them.

"So your government could hold the plane as security that they will pay the fines and legal costs?" suggested Boma, smiling. Again, there was silence behind the bars.

"We have not finished questioning them," stated Mulama.

"You questioned us for over an hour without permitting us to call a lawyer," said one of the Americans.

Ben asked Mulama, "May I speak to the suspects?"

"In my presence," came the reply.

"Gentlemen, I spent four years in the United States, so I can appreciate the U.S. legal system under which one is innocent until proven guilty. Please understand that under a Napoleonic legal system in force in Miseria you are guilty until you prove yourself innocent. And lack of cooperation with legal authorities is itself a crime even if you are innocent."

Ben noted the Americans looked perplexed, so he tried to raise their spirits. "Here is the best lawyer in Miseria, Mr. Boma." Boma smiled. "And the most highly experienced police officer, who is also solving the murder last Saturday of our colleague, Dr. Xavier Hudunu. For your own sakes and the sake of Hudunu's family, please cooperate with these men in their work."

By now the Californians looked chastened, and Boma and Mulama felt vindicated.

"Will you release the men with our guarantee of legal compensation?" asked Ben. Boma smiled.

"There is also the matter of the cameras," added Mulama.

"Video?" asked Boma.

"We found two sophisticated still cameras and a video-camera when we searched the plane. We are examining them to see if they were used for spying."

"That's my Nikon and his Zeiss and Sony Camcorder," said one of the Americans.

"We cannot release the Americans if they are spies." Ben suspected that Mulama wished to confiscate the valuable equipment for himself.

"If you hold the film and videotapes, you could review them at your convenience while they attend the conference." Apparently Boma wanted to give Mulama the film without the cameras.

"Not our film! We need it for the conference!" yelled the other American.

Ben wanted to stop the protest before he lost everything. "We can buy more film and videotape in the capital to use while the police are examining yours. If you stay here, you won't attend the conference," he pointed out.

Mulama looked pleased with himself. "We will examine the film and permit them to use their cameras, provided they obey the laws of the land."

"Thank you," said Ben and Boma in unison.

Mulama ordered the guard to open the jail door.

"My name is Dr. Benjamin Mchunguzi Maluum. I'm the conference organizer." He shook their hands.

"Pleased to meet you. I'm Francis Falco," said one.

"Thank you for coming. I'm Paul Piccione," said the other.

They shook hands dutifully with Mulama and Boma.

Ben thanked Mulama and wished him well in the Hudunu

case. He invited him to the conference reception Wednesday evening. Mulama's eyes widened as he accepted Ben's good wishes.

Mulama turned to the Americans. "Go into the reception hall and finish Immigration and Customs formalities." The Americans stiffened but held their tongues.

As they left, Ben whispered, "Please declare all of your U.S. currency down to the penny. The officials need only the smallest excuse to confiscate all your money."

"I understand," said Falco grimly. They cleared Customs quickly without mishap.

Boma's chauffeur brought the Mercedes and loaded the trunk with their matched sets of suitcases. They started back to the capital.

Ben observed, "That was a long trip. I am glad you will have a day to recover."

"Yes, but not as long as commercial flights through Europe," crowed Falco. "We flew from California to Washington, D.C. Then I decided this trip was going so well I didn't need to take a commercial jet." He added excitedly, "I calculated that with the new fuel tanks and favorable weather we could avoid the delays of waiting in those departure lounges. So we went to the Canary Islands, refueled, and then flew here."

"The Canary Islands are under Spanish jurisdiction and have laws about overflights."

"Don't worry. They love tourists, and U.S. dollars talk."

"Is this your first flight outside the United States?"

"No, I go down to Mexico regularly."

"Do you ever have difficulties with Immigration or the Drug Enforcement Administration?"

"No. They know me at the airport. I'm not doing anything wrong."

"How much did the fuel cost for the flight?"

"Only about the same cost as two airline tickets. I would burn the fuel anyway to get my flying time."

Boma saw his opportunity. "Speaking of money, I will require a bank transfer wired to my European account in the amount of $500 for my services."

"That is pretty expensive even by American standards," snapped Falco.

"I left my other work and spent an hour to free you. It will cost more hours to free your plane. Are your freedom and your plane worth $500?"

"This is robbery! Will you let him do that to me?" he asked, glaring at Ben.

Ben looked back at him. "I presume that some of that money will serve to convince officials in five countries to drop charges and permit you to fly back. If Mr. Boma can assure you of those advantages, I would consider the price quite reasonable."

"You should help me get reasonable prices for legal services."

"I came to get you out of jail, not to talk to your lawyer about the cost of legal services. But remember your plane is worth more than $500!"

"Wait a moment!" Falco shot back. "I did not hire this guy who is gouging me. You did! You pay him."

Ben glowered at him. "I recognize that you are upset over the hostile reception and added expenses for your trip. Your decision to fly yourself was a dangerous and expensive one. The conference was only responsible for meeting you, which we did."

Turning to the lawyer, Falco refused to give up. "Still, we never signed a contract with you specifying the cost of your services."

"I signed a release form to assure legal responsibility for you. If I cancel my support, you will have to find another lawyer to get your release," Boma stated firmly. "We will stop at my office, so you can telex your bank."

The Mercedes zig-zagged around potholes. Falco looked miserable. "I should never have come!"

Piccione said quietly, "It seemed like fun to fly ourselves, but maybe we should have taken the commercial flight after all."

Ben spoke soothingly, "Both of you look exhausted. Wait until you have a good lunch and nap before you decide your future plans." Changing the subject, he asked Boma, "Is Mulama an effective investigator for solving Professor Hudunu's murder?"

"I think so," said Boma. "I was discussing it with him yesterday evening at the President's reception. He said he has questioned the suspects and is considering his next move."

Ben hoped he was not a suspect. "Are there political implications to the case?"

"Perhaps so. Hudunu may have been plotting to overthrow the government," replied Boma.

"Do university professors have any power in Miseria?"

"Some of his former students are highly placed in government service."

"Since the government has to trim its payroll and balance its budget in order to comply with International Monetary Fund stipulations, might this issue become a pretext to dismiss civil servants?"

"I see you are familiar with Miserian politics," observed Boma.

"No, I am not. But I have seen it happen elsewhere."

Back at the hotel Ben found the student assistants waiting patiently for him. With them he reviewed the conference schedule assigning each to lead a tour group. Feeling confident of their abilities he dismissed them.

New problems had emerged for Ben. A telegram indicated that the chairman of the first panel missed his flight and would be a day late. Fortunately, Karla Curmudgeon was on hand. He would ask her to take the chair. Two delegates from Ivory Coast objected to their accommodations and moved to the American hotel. A copying machine on loan from the University had not arrived. A minor official objected to removing it from university premises. Ben tried to reach Dean Gomez by telephone, but the calls did not get through. A welcome piece of good news came from the engineering professor at the University, who called Ben to inform him that eighty-two earphone sets were operational. He would transport the translating equipment when the technicians had been paid.

Ben jumped into a taxi and sped to the University. He paid 320 bars to the lab technician and made gifts of 150 bars to his helper and two students. They signed receipts and helped load the translation equipment into his taxi. The technician accompanied him to the Dean's office. A quick phone call secured release of the copying machine. The lab technician collected it and loaded it into the taxi. Together they returned to the hotel, where Ben paid the taxi driver and the porters to move the equipment into the grand ballroom.

He sent a note to the hotel manager requesting that the staff set up tables and chairs so the technician could install the translation equipment. He gave the technician two bars to purchase lunch from the women vendors on the street and waited for him to return. Four cleaning men arrived and started sweeping out the hall and mopping the tile floor. They worked in unison, singing together under the direction of the eldest. Their good spirits charmed Ben and made him forget for a moment the problems of organizing the conference.

Once the technicians returned, Ben directed the arrangement of the tables. He left the technician stringing wires and testing equipment and the staff setting up chairs. In his room, he called Curmudgeon's room and asked her to chair the first panel, a request she accepted.

As Ben descended the stairs to the dining hall, the front

desk clerk gave him a message to call Dean Gomez. Though he called his office and home, Gomez was not there.

At lunch he joined Curmudgeon and Pedant. They had a merry time recalling the foibles of their colleagues. Ben refrained from telling them of the morning's crisis with the Californians, who did not come to the dining hall.

After lunch he found the Californians in the bar drinking heavily. He greeted them and shared a beer while he tried to guess their next crisis. They had shed their beards and smelly clothes, but their childish attitude remained. They tried to buy respect by lavishing drinks on everyone present. The bar was full of hangers-on and several women flattered them in hopes of money. The scene disgusted Ben, who fled as soon as he finished his beer.

In the room he reached Dean Gomez, who was distraught. "The chemistry professor called this morning to tell me that he performed atomic absorption spectroscopy and found the sample contained heavy metals. Mercury causes liver toxicity. Lead and cadmium do neurological damage and eventually cause paralysis. He identifies it as incinerator ash."

"Are there waste incinerators in Miseria?" asked Ben.

"No. It had to be imported."

"That violates the 1988 resolution of the Organization of African Unity against toxic waste imports into Africa and the 1989 U.N. convention on toxic waste trade."

"Yes. Someone in Miseria is violating the law. I called the Ministry of Health, where they informed me that the danger of contact on the skin is minor. However, if the toxic chemicals are not washed off the hands before eating, then the waste could be hazardous."

"The Miserian practice is to wash right hands in a common bowl and eat with them," observed Ben.

"Yes. Our eating habits make us vulnerable. I called the Ministry of Foreign Commerce to warn them about smuggling. I also called the Ministry of the Interior, which is responsible for regulating traditional markets, so that they would confiscate stocks of the industrial ash."

"Well, we may have done more for Miseria by exposing this problem than we will by holding an economics conference."

"Maybe so. But if Hudunu found this problem too, we may also be threatening powerful people. Please do not take a midnight walk on the beach, Ben. We need you!"

"From now on I won't leave the hotel."

"Good. I will come by this evening."

Ben lay down for a siesta in his safari suit, but thoughts prevented him from sleeping. Someone was importing toxic waste to earn foreign exchange. That person distributed it through the network of traditional medicine sellers. Were government officials involved in the importation and distribution? Hudunu's interest in traditional markets might have led him to discover the situation. If so, clearly the murderer was not a traditional medicine seller with access to "other means of silencing him." Was a foreigner or a government official familiar with the Western murder methods involved?

Ben phoned the Hudunu home hoping to learn if the professor had discovered the white stones. The line was busy. A soft knock sounded at his door. He froze. "Who is it?"

"Miss Ilena Hudunu."

He opened the door.

"Dean Gomez says you must leave now. The chemistry professor was questioned by police and Felipe was arrested. They are tapping phones."

Ben realized that the Ministry of the Interior was involved. "I'm coming." He grabbed his shoulder bag.

"My boyfriend is at the side door. His motorbike is outside on the beach. Change shirts with him and take the bike. We will go to the grill to watch the lobby."

Ben gave her a fifty-bar note. "For your expenses. Stay away from the two Americans in the bar." He found the boyfriend outside the door and changed shirts with him. The young man handed him a key.

"Ride toward the coconut plantation and take the first path to the right. Go half a kilometer and you will arrive at a village. Ask for the home of Francisco Gomez. Good luck."

"Thank you. How will you get your motorbike back?"

"He will guard it for me." The boy went inside.

Ben sauntered nonchalantly toward the gate, hoping to look inconspicuous in his simple print shirt. He wore his shoulder bag on the side away from the dining room, so the monogram would not give him away. The bike was leaning against the wall. Ben put in the key, pedaled it, turned the clutch, and hoped it would start. To his relief, it did.

He was glad he had ridden a friend's motorcycle in the United States. He rode close to the wall, where the sand seemed the hardest. Then he picked a route where some grass offered traction. The machine rocked and bucked under him. In meeting this challenge he did not realize that he drove over the sand dune where Hudunu's body had been found. The bike slithered down the face of the sand dune to the hard sand by the ocean. There he straightened up and moved quickly. The wind whipped at him. He looked back at the hotel, but could see no one pursuing him.

The beach was deserted. Ben remembered the British song from India, "Only mad dogs and Englishmen go out in the noonday sun."

He realized that from the oceanside he could not see any paths through the coconut groves. He guessed, though, that the children this morning would have come from the first village. When he reached the point where he remembered those children, he plunged back up the beach. Sure enough, as the motor sputtered under him, he spotted a path of hard sand through the coconut palms. With some desperate pushing, he reached the path. The motor roared through the still air under the palms.

Presently he arrived at the village. Most of the inhabitants were inside during the noon siesta. He saw a grey-haired man talking to a woman balancing a water bucket on her head. She turned and left, rhythmically swaying under her load. Ben slowed to greet the man, "Good afternoon, sir. Where does Francisco Gomez live?"

"I am Francisco Gomez. Are you Dr. Mchunguzi?"

"I am."

"Follow that woman with the bucket. Watch where she turns into her house. Continue on the path to the lagoon. Leave the bike where the canoes land. Return on foot to her house. Do not contact me again, since the walls have ears here."

Ben did as he was directed. He saw her enter some mud-brick walls toward a run-down thatched hut. After passing a dozen other housing compounds, he arrived at a murky lagoon. He parked the bike next to some canoes and walked back to the place where the woman had entered the compound. He approached without a greeting, so as not to disturb the inhabitants. The woman motioned him to enter the hut. He wondered if onlookers would interpret their furtive movements as carrying on an affair. In an African village he could count on onlookers.

Inside the hut, darkness prevented him from seeing much. He whispered, "Good afternoon. Thank you for inviting me."

"You are welcome. Papa Gomez told me shelter you."

"My name is Professor Mchunguzi."

"My name, Francesca. My husband, Salvador."

Ben had not noticed a figure lying on the double bed in the corner. "I am pleased to meet you."

Salvador wheezed and replied, "You are welcome."

Francesca set up a chair by the bed. Ben sat down. "Are you suffering, old man?"

Salvador looked at him. "You how old, Dr. Mchunguzi?"

Ben straightened, "I am forty-six years old."

He wheezed again. "I have fifty-two years. In this village we are in the same age group."

"I am sorry. I could not see you properly." He noticed Salvador's gaunt look and wondered if he had AIDS. "Are you suffering?"

"Yes. My chest not working. I was welder with Miserian Electrical Authority. The smoke hurt my lungs."

Francesca brought in Cokes and two glasses. She poured the liquid.

"Did the company give you a pension?"

"Yes. But small small."

Ben looked at his surroundings and agreed. "Where did you work?"

"I work power pylons, hydro dam, and boiler."

"What province did you work in?"

"I work in Northern province, then Sodu province."

"Where did you live in Sodu?"

"I live in civil service house. What country come from, Professor?"

"I come from Kenya to organize a meeting about economic development with Dean Gomez."

"I know Dean Gomez. He is young brother of Francisco, at University."

"We found poison products from Europe. Traditional healers sell poison products to people. The police came to arrest one man who found the poison. So Dean Gomez told me to go to his brother."

"Good, you are welcome. We hide you here when police come."

Ben was amazed at the man's trust and courage.

"Did the police come when Professor Hudunu was murdered?"

"Yes. They want take me to beach. I say no. They beat me." He moved uncomfortably. "Everybody cry and ask pardon. Then some say I have slim, AIDS. So they go fast. They not come back."

Ben smiled. He could visualize the drama. A harassed policeman trying to obey orders to walk the elders to the beach. "You are a brave man. Do you have medicine for your chest?"

Salvador showed Ben an inhaler and some bottles. The names on them were complicated and meant nothing to him. "Is the medicine expensive?"

"Very expensive," Salvador said earnestly.

Ben saw that he could repay the man by helping to buy him medicine.

"Was your work hard?"

"Very hard! On pylons we live in camps in the bush. No wives to cook for us. We work in rain and sun. Some men killed by lightning when we work in rainy season."

"I am sorry."

"Much better for hydro dam. Government build village. We work each day. There are roads. We can leave. But only one dam is made. Then government has no money. For Sodu life in boiler room is very hard. Hot building, not much fans. I breathe smoke. Like hell. Make me sick."

"I am sorry. Is your family from Sodu?"

"No, from here."

"How did you travel here?"

"By launch from Sodu to port or by canoe on lagoon."

"So the lagoon goes from here behind the capital to Sodu?"

"Yes, to Sodu."

Ben realized that the swamp they passed over on the way to Hudu was crisscrossed by creeks accessible to canoes. He could visit Sodu by passing the capital if he chose to.

"Were there many smugglers in Sodu?"

"Too many! Every night canoes go out. They meet ships at night near capital, bring back everything cheap." He smiled.

"Who were the smugglers?"

"Rich people and Europeans." He wheezed.

"Did the Customs officials permit smugglers?"

"Officials eat money. Sometimes they catch them and eat more money."

Screams came from the lane outside. Salvador quickly gave instructions, "Crawl under bed. Police coming." He hid their glasses under his bedcover and slid the bottles behind himself.

Ben had the presence of mind to find his shoulder bag and push it under the bed first. The floor was damp and smelled like mold. Hoping not to sneeze, he pulled himself through the maze of spider webs under Salvador's bed.

Footsteps arrived in the compound. Salvador wheezed nervously. The screams outside showed the police had searched the women's quarters first. Without warning two policemen burst through the door and stopped as Salvador coughed. "Where is he?" one shouted.

"Who?" replied Salvador weakly.

"The alien!"

"What alien?"

"The alien who came here."

Salvador struggled with another cough. "No alien come here."

The policemen's boots shifted. "Who bring chair?"

"Wife bring to sit," said Salvador smoothly. Ben was grateful that Coca-Cola did not have an odor that would give him away, like alcohol.

There was silence. "We punish you if he came." Another silence. They turned and left the room. Screams came from other compounds.

Finally a Landrover started up the lane. The screams ended. Francesca returned. "Police go."

Ben crawled out from under the bed. "Thank you. You saved me."

Both of them were smiling.

Ben tried to wipe the dirt off his clothing. Francesca scurried out to find a bowl of water and a towel.

Francisco Gomez entered quietly and surprised them. "How are you?" he asked, shaking their hands.

Ben waited for Salvador to answer, then replied, "I'm fine. You saved me."

"Yes. Police threaten in my compound. No one know you are here, so no one say."

Ben winced. "Does Dean Gomez know I am here?"

"Yes. I send before daughter to him with letter."

Salvador brought out the glasses and bottles from hiding. "We drink your safety." Francesca handed him another glass and placed a bowl of water before Ben, who washed while Salvador poured Coke in the glasses.

Ben took one. "To the brave people of this village," he said sincerely.

"God protects us," said Francisco, in a tone just like his younger brother. "Canoeman see police. He drive moto away to capital. Police find moto go. They go. They cannot catch him."

They all laughed, then sipped triumphantly.

Ben realized that Dean Gomez was right. The police would search for him. They must have learned about his escape by motorbike, which meant Hudunu's daughter and friend were in danger too. He wondered how he would leave Miseria now and what would happen to the others.

Francisco excused himself, "I must go. No one know you here." He shook hands with Ben and Salvador.

Ben asked, "What time is the news on the radio?"

"Six o'clock," came the reply. Salvador pointed to a battered old transistor radio by his bed. "Please, listen."

"Not now." Ben hoped the batteries would work when the time came. "The smugglers in Sodu have what names?"

"So many names."

"Cartagena?"

"No."

"Traficant?"

"Yes."

"What others?"

"Taajir and Lusoos."

"Which are Africans?"

"Plenty Africans."

"Sodunu?"

"Yes."

"Is Corporal Sodunu in the police from the smugglers' family?"

"Yes."

"Does he eat money from smugglers?"

"From others. Not from family."

"From Traficant?"

"Yes."

"Does Traficant sell medicine?"

"No."

"Does Sodunu family sell medicine?"

"Yes, in market."

"Other African smugglers, do they sell medicine in market?"

"Gana family."

"Do they have police or Customs officials in family?"

"No."

The evidence was circumstantial. The Sodunu family could import industrial ash and distribute it through medicine sellers. With a few precautions they would be safe from its effects. Traficant could help them. When Hudunu discovered them, the Sodunus could have murdered him. Corporal Sodunu would cover-up the crime for his family. He could mobilize police to arrest Felipe and raid the village. If the cover up extended to Mulama or the Minister of the Interior, Ben would be publicly declared a murderer by the Miserian

National Radio. He wondered how his hosts would treat him if that happened.

"I must journey to Sodu by canoe."

"Tomorrow. No canoe tonight, only ferry."

Ben did not want to return to the capital to take a public ferry. "Tomorrow is fine."

A little boy arrived and handed a letter to Salvador, who nodded and dismissed him. "Gomez daughter son," he explained to Ben and handed him the note.

Dear Ben,

I am happy to hear that you are safe. I asked my brother to expect you and hide you, if there is danger.

We are well. My messengers left after you and before police arrived at the hotel. Police questioned my family, the Hudunu family, and university students to find you. Corporal Sodunu commands them.

I retrieved your files before he confiscated them. They are helpful. Dossou and I have postponed our work to prepare the beginning of the conference tomorrow. We are careful not to be caught alone.

Remember God watches you in this time of trial.

Gomez

P.S. Please burn this note.

Ben explained, "Dean Gomez is well. The police questioned his family. Corporal Sodunu leads them."

"Sodunu bad family," said Salvador philosophically. He tuned the radio, and they listened to African music.

Ben wondered if Francesca and Salvador were following normal routines so their neighbors would not suspect a foreign visitor. He knew he could not keep his presence a secret long in such a tight-knit village. He admired their fortitude in accepting two police raids in less than a week, but he wondered how long their solidarity would last in the face of police oppression.

Presently Miserian news began. The President of Miseria sent a letter to Zimbabwe congratulating it on the anniversary of its independence. He received the German ambassador, who brought an important message from his government. The Minister of Health opened a clinic for the diagnosis and treatment of cancer at the University Hospital. The Miserian national cycling team left for Senegal to participate in a race. Two Americans were briefly detained at the airport for violations of international flight rules. They were released after authorities questioned them and inspected their aircraft.

For Ben the news was good. First, the government appeared stable on the eve of his conference. Next, even if curative medicine were less cost-effective than preventive medicine in Miseria, in this case the cancer clinic might help alleviate the consequences of the industrial ash. It might also have equipment to help Salvador. The lawyer Boma had apparently done his job. Falco and Piccione had not been charged with any wrongdoing. Most importantly, Ben was not publicly a fugitive.

International news was also reassuring. Another conference started to help fight the menace of locusts in Africa. A protest by Africans about the world debt situation. More talks on the future of Eastern Europe. Announcement of a new AIDS treatment that would not require hospitalization.

Again Ben was relieved to hear of no plane crashes, hijackings, or disputes between nations represented at the conference. He realized that he had not adopted the mentality of a fugitive. Instead, he still belonged to the world of public gatherings. He worried if his reflexes were appropriate for the trials he would face.

Francesca brought in dinner. She had boiled some yams and fixed a vegetable sauce to go with them. Hot pepper spiced it. As a treat for Ben she brought a small can of sardines. The family ate meat only on special occasions. She handed Ben a tin plate with a spoon and Salvador just a plate, then she left. After blessing their meal, Salvador ate with his fingers in silence.

The meal was filling at least. The hot pepper went to Ben's nose, which had stuffed up while he was under the bed. He realized with regret that he did not have any medicine — decongestant, aspirin, or even anti-malarial tablets — with him. If he asked his hosts for medicine, they would scurry around to find it, bothering people and making them suspicious. He would have to hold out.

Francesca came back to clear up. She took Ben's note to burn. Salvador's son came by after work to give him news. The two spoke rapidly in a local language without referring to Ben, who had no idea how his presence would be explained. Eventually the son's two children entered with Francesca. They approached their grandfather, who patted them with great affection. They also shook Ben's hand gravely and then left with their father.

Shortly another man arrived. Salvador introduced him as a cousin named Pedro, who would take Ben in a canoe to Sodu. They would leave at dawn. Though the man spoke only a little Spanish, his children would accompany them to translate. Again, Ben was grateful to the family. He explained that in order to blend in with other travelers he wished to exchange his city clothes and shoes for a used local outfit of matching African shirt and pants and a pair of sandals. While they went to get the clothes, he peeled the monogram off his shoulder bag, tore the Kenyan labels out of his pants, and scratched at the British writing in his shoes. For everyone's sake he would be wiser to burn any evidence linking them to him, but the state of poverty among his protectors made him give the clothes away. Although the family returned with an outfit newer and more stylish than he wished, he dared not refuse their gift. They were pleased to receive "European" products in exchange.

Ben also offered Salvador most of his small notes in bars

to help him pay for his medicine. It was the least he could do for people taking such risks for him. The sick man gravely accepted the gift of 120 bars, as if it were an act of great generosity on Ben's part, when actually it only represented his small bills. He dared not leave any one-hundred-bar notes, believing they would give away his presence.

A young high school student arrived with some mathematics problems that he was studying by the light of a storm lantern. He wanted advice from "the Professor." Ben realized that his identity was now current knowledge throughout the village. He was relieved that he would disappear early in the morning, so his hosts would no longer be in danger.

Francesca arrived with a reed sleeping mat half an inch thick to protect Ben from the damp floor. She offered him a bowl of water, home-made soap, and a towel to wash with. Salvador gave Ben a large African cloth for sleeping. Then he said a prayer for the safety of the three of them and for Ben on his journey. Ben rolled up in the cloth, covering his head and feet to protect himself from mosquitoes, which were already biting exposed parts of his body.

Chapter V

The Trickster

☙

BEN WAS AWAKE AND MISERABLE before Francesca started moving around in the courtyard to prepare the fire. He had sweated and itched all night. He wanted a shower but did not want to disturb Salvador, who was sleeping peacefully. He dressed quietly for the trip and shaved with cold wash water from the night before. Eventually Francesca entered with hot tea and a loaf of bread for his breakfast. He noticed with regret that she also brought warm wash water. While she waited, he ate in silence, wishing he could listen to the radio in order to check the political situation.

After he finished, she led him down to the landing where a large canoe waited. He met the canoeman, a huge jolly fellow, and the other passengers: a muscular youth, Salvador's cousin Pedro, his wife, and their two sons. After the greetings Pedro said a prayer for their trip. They all stepped into the canoe.

Ben said goodbye to Francesca and shook her hand. He seated himself with the family. The canoeman pushed off solidly and poled the craft out into the shallow lagoon. The canoe was large, too large to have been hollowed from a tree. Trained boatmakers had built it of planks sealed with tar. It had smooth lines and an outboard motor, Ben was happy to note. He whispered to Pedro, "Does the motor work?"

"Yes," came the reply. "It work soon."

Ben could see the track leading from the village in the direction of the capital. "Where does the road go?" he asked.

"To capital. Soon road turn and motor work."

"The canoeman on the motorbike, did he come back?"

"Yes, fine." Pedro glanced at the canoeman. "He is the one."

Ben smiled appreciatively. "Where is the motorbike?"

"Last night Francisco daughter take motorbike and letter to Dean Gomez."

Ben marveled at the extent of organization in the village. He recalled stories from his region of Kenya in the 1950s, when the villagers had organized the Land and People Army against the British colonialists. Women had served valiantly alongside the men, carrying supplies and information to the fighters in the forest. For that they had to bear collective punishments and concentration camps.

The canoeman slid the boat into high grass as a vehicle came along the track. It was a pickup with benches in back for workers going early to the coconut plantations and others from villages going to the capital. Soon the swampy area became thicker on both sides of the lagoon, and they could no longer see the road.

The canoeman began to tinker with the motor. He poured some fuel mixture into the carburetor and twisted the throttle experimentally. He tilted the motor. He inspected a homemade starting cord thoroughly, then wrapped it around the top. He yanked on the cord and leapt backward at the same time. The motor sputtered. He repeated the ritual. Ben hoped the starting cord would not break or they would capsize. The canoeman smiled grimly to the passengers and declared hopefully, "Motor go!" He leaped again, the motor caught, he dived back and wiggled the throttle. Blue smoke poured out the back of the motor. The canoeman turned the clutch and the canoe slipped quickly through the water.

The passengers began to talk merrily together. The children inspected Ben gravely. He asked their names.

"Pablo and Fidel," replied Fidel.

"Where did you learn Spanish?"

"In school."

"Which grade?"

"Fourth for me and third for him," answered Fidel, with the authority of the eldest. Pablo translated so that the others could follow the conversation with the stranger.

"Is your school in the village?"

"No, we go to school in the capital."

"Do you walk every day?" They both giggled at the question.

"No. Uncle is a school teacher. We stayed with his family."

"How many children stay with him?"

Ben was amused as they listed their names rather than answering with a statistic.

"Eleven," Fidel concluded.

"How many were born to the school teacher?"

"Five."

"And the rest are relatives?"

"Yes."

"How many students are in your class?"

"Fifty-eight." They knew that statistic. "Do all the classes have that many?"

"Some have more students. Some have fewer."

Their grammar was good for such an overcrowded school. "Do all the children come every day?"

"No, some are sick. They do not have notebooks or pencils or a uniform. So they do not come. Some help with family work."

"Do you and Pablo go to school every day?"

"Yes," they both answered eagerly.

"Today you are not in school," Ben observed.

"No, we must translate for the Professor," they replied proudly.

"Thank you," said Ben. "I am happy to talk to you." He wished he could give them a spare notebook that he carried from the University of Nairobi but did not dare incriminate them. Back at the hotel he also kept some Kenya tourism T-shirts for such occasions.

"Do you also learn the vernacular language in your school?"

They looked at each other with surprise. Pablo answered, "We speak Spanish all the time at school."

"Do you speak Spanish at home too?"

"Uncle speaks it to us. Unless he is angry!"

Ben laughed. "And Auntie?"

"No, she speaks Miserian dialect."

"Can she speak Spanish?"

"She learned a little in school, but she does not speak it. She does not want to be embarrassed."

"Are people who do not know Spanish embarrassed in Miseria?"

"Of course." They smiled assuredly.

"In Kenya we learn Swahili, an African language, in school. Our lessons are in Swahili, and we study English to prepare for secondary studies."

"But can you speak Swahili throughout Kenya?"

"Of course. We can speak Swahili in neighboring countries too: Uganda, Tanzania, Rwanda, Burundi, and even parts of Zaire. Do you know those countries?"

They answered "Yes. We learn about them in geography."

"Do you speak Miserian dialect throughout Miseria?"

"No. It is the language of the capital province. Only people who have lived in the capital understand it."

"What language do people speak in the markets?"

"They speak the local vernacular."

"Can you understand the vernacular of Hudu and Sodu?"

"A little from Sodu, because my grandfather was there," answered Fidel.

"I also speak Hudu, because my classmate is from there," chimed in Pablo.

"Which vernacular languages do the elders speak?" asked Ben.

The boys questioned them gravely. Their parents each spoke three, the youth two, and the canoeman claimed five local languages, "because he is in transportation." The canoeman knew a little Spanish, although he had followed Pablo's translation of the conversation with the boys.

Ben asked them to say "This canoe goes fast" in each language. They repeated the sentence for him with great enjoyment. He noted differences in vocabulary between Hudu and the capital. He was not sure what the pronunciation differences were between the dialects of Sodu and the capital.

In several cases they disagreed on the words chosen. Then Ben asked for "This canoe went fast" and "This canoe will go fast." Apparently the present tense, "The canoe goes fast," in the local languages was more complicated than whichever past tense they used: "The canoe went fast" or "The canoe was going fast" or possibly "The canoe continued to go fast." They all debated enthusiastically how to answer each question by "the Professor."

Through this simple exercise Ben gained new respect for linguists trying to sort out the meaning of a single sentence. He made a mental note to ask Biggles or a Miserian linguist about the local languages.

Out of pride that his canoe was the object of such distinguished interest, the canoeman opened up the throttle. The canoe shot through the creek very "fast."

Ben noticed that the canoe had to maneuver through rows of poles forming a V-shape in the water. The structures alternated sides of the creek where the current flowed deepest, so the canoeman had to slalom to avoid them. He asked the canoeman. "What are these?"

"Catch fish," came the reply.

He spotted a mesh trap bobbing at the end. They passed dugout canoes with fishermen harvesting their catch. The men did not seem perturbed to see a motorized canoe careen through their fishing zone.

At high speed they surprised some young women bathing. The canoe caused consternation as the modest women grabbed cloths or sank in the dark water. The passengers laughed good-naturedly. The youth gestured lasciviously in the bow, while the canoeman yelled something for their enjoyment. Ben asked for the translation, which was "Women should bathe before dawn or after cooking." Apparently he had no qualms about interrupting lazy village belles at midmorning.

Ben spoke to the canoeman as Fidel translated, "When I said 'The canoe goes fast,' I was not requesting that the canoe go faster. I do not want the canoeman to waste fuel." He neglected to add "or burn out his motor."

The canoeman replied, "I am happy to show good motor to the Professor from Kenya." He then lowered the throttle to cruising speed.

"Where is the capital?" Ben asked, to keep conversation going.

The canoeman pointed southward.

"Do police come to the lagoon?"

"Bridge," came the reply.

Ben worried about the road across the swamp with the police barrier at the bridge. He noticed the passengers began singing together. He thought he could make out the tune to "Nearer My God to Thee" and "Hallelujah, Praise Ye the Lord." He wondered if they were tense about the bridge too.

The canoeman kept looking ahead, apparently unruffled by the prospect of a police check. In the distance they saw the causeway for the road across the swamp. Their canoe proceeded toward it. They could see a line of buses and trucks parked for inspection at the roadblock before the bridge. Police were looking at identity papers, opening bags, and sliding prods into bags of food.

Ben noticed that a stairway led from the end of the bridge down to the creek. A cement platform at the bottom had tie-ups for boats, so the police could easily come down and inspect the cargo. As the boat approached a policeman hailed them in Spanish from the bridge. He demanded, "What cargo do you have?"

The canoeman idled the motor. "No cargo, only people." Ben squinted up at him, trying to look like he was ignorant of the language.

"Show me their bags," ordered the policeman. The others pulled out their travel bags and Ben held up a bundle wrapped in a bandana. If Ben were ordered to open it, the files would attract suspicion.

"Open the woman's bag," said the policeman. She opened it and pulled out a change of clothes and some bags of food.

"Are they all Miserians?" asked the policeman.

"Yes," declared the canoeman, and they all nodded in unison.

"Go!" ordered the policeman.

The canoeman revved the motor and slid under the bridge. Without looking back they continued through the swamp. The canoeman laughed. "Police too lazy! Not look in canoe."

The others joined in with stories about villages outsmarting the authorities. Fidel and Pablo took turns translating them for Ben.

At one point in the conversation Pedro looked at Ben and said prophetically, "You are the Trickster!"

"Who is the Trickster?" Ben asked, thinking they were mocking him.

"The Spider is the Trickster." That confused him.

Fidel explained, "In our stories the Spider always fools the Crocodile or the Hyena."

"How?"

"They are too proud, and he is too wise. Just like you!"

"How do you know I am wise and not proud?"

"Because you teach at University and you travel with us too."

"I am happy to travel with you." Ben smiled. "And I learn things from you too."

"You do?" They were incredulous.

"Yes, I learn the story of the Spider. We do not have such a story in Kenya. Why do you call him the Trickster too?"

"No one knows when he will surprise them and reveal their true heart," answered Pablo.

Ben followed the reasoning. "How does he surprise them?"

"All the time he tests people. He puts a doll covered with honey in front of a greedy man. The man takes it and sticks to it."

"I see."

"He comes naked in front of a woman." They giggled.

"Why?"

"To frighten her!"

"Why would he want to frighten her?"

"To test her."

"Would you want him to frighten your mother? Ask your mother."

They did. She laughed. Pablo translated her reply. "Don't worry. Men's nakedness would not frighten me."

"We frightened the women who were bathing."

"Yes," they chortled. "The mate made the Trickster's sign at them."

Ben remained perplexed. "If he made the sign, why does the canoeman say I am the Trickster?"

Fidel translated the canoeman's reply, "Because you appeared before the policeman and he was lazy, so he did not see you."

Ben dropped the subject. Apparently they understood as well as he did the game he was playing with the authorities. Their explanation in African folk tales was as sophisticated as his in Western social science. With a language barrier, he could not fully comprehend the many meanings of their tale. He resolved to ask a Miserian anthropologist to translate for him the meaning of the Spider stories.

As the tropical rain forest reached out over the creeks, Ben asked, "Are there smugglers in these creeks?"

"Yes, plenty," answered the canoeman.

"Do they rob canoes?"

"Yes, sometimes."

The other passengers grew silent. Ben hesitated, "Have they robbed you?"

"Yes, they rob me," he answered.

The woman reached over and pointed at a leather nail file case protruding from Ben's bundle. She said something to Pablo, who translated, "She says, 'You are strong. You brought a gun.' "

Ben looked down at the bundle and saw that it looked like the holster in a cowboy movie. He realized they would feel safer if he pretended to carry a gun, so he replied, "I am glad the policeman did not ask me to open my bundle."

"So are we!" they answered.

Ben tried to put confidence in his posture. It was difficult, since in the shade of the rain forest mosquitos attacked them viciously. While air movement around the canoe protected Ben's head and arms, the mosquitoes took advantage of the still air in the hull to attack his feet. The others seemed to accept the torment philosophically, but Ben wiggled his feet in rhythm to deter the insects. He realized he was losing the battle when he found blood as he slapped his ankles.

For the first time since arriving in Miseria, he had time to think. Twenty-four hours ago he shed responsibility for the economics conference when he went into hiding. Conference details became the concerns of Dean Gomez, Dossou, and Rosa.

Yesterday morning he worried about two Americans flying in from the United States. Today he worried about not becoming a pirate's prize in a Miserian swamp.

His quest was to find Hudunu's murderer, expose any accomplices, and free himself from pursuit by the Miserian police. To do so he approached the heartland of Miserian smuggling without a clear plan of action.

His major asset now was anonymity. Apparently the police at the bridge did not expect that he would use such a humble conveyance as a native canoe. His ability to identify with common people gave him invisibility from the elite. He could reconnoiter Sodu and decide his next move then.

He remembered his childhood in the countryside in the hill country in Kenya. He too had gone to a village elementary school started by the mission. He was fortunate, though, to win a scholarship to the Presbyterian boarding school in Kikuyu. Only one other boy from his village school had a chance for a secondary education with assistance from relatives like Pablo and Fidel did. Ben successfully passed the entrance examinations and joined the privileged few who went to university.

As a college professor, he always took a special interest in students from rural backgrounds. They had more difficulties adjusting to the individualism and thought processes taught in a Western-style education. They had to reconcile themselves with the traditional culture, like the Spider stories, in which they grew up.

In graduate school, Hudunu had challenged Ben to integrate economic reasoning and African thought. By then Ben looked forward to his career in a university. He was proud of his mastery of the economic logic. Individual material success seemed natural. Hudunu maintained that in Africa communal land tenure and collective celebration meant that the preference function must include building up the community before personal satisfaction. In response to Hudunu's challenge, Ben decided to take a leave of absence in order to launch the African Regional Program for the World Economics Association, though Ben was happy and secure in his position at the University of Nairobi.

As he sat in the heat and mosquitoes, Ben noticed that his fellow passengers were putting his safety above their own comfort. He reflected with gratitude on their sense of community, which led them to protect him from his enemies despite the cost.

Eventually they passed clearings. Farmers had cut and cleared the thick forest for their fields, an enormous job considering the size of the trees. As on the plateau the fields grew a mixture of crops. Ben noticed that here the land did not look spent as it sometimes did on the plateau, where farmers could plant only manioc. Apparently it had grown crops for years without being abandoned to the bush in order to regenerate the soil. He asked, "Do farmers here use fertilizer?"

"No, every year the floods in the rainy season leave fresh dirt on the fields."

The dark water that churned up slime as the motor passed over it held riches for the land.

In one clearing they found a small village. The canoeman slid his craft up the shore and announced it was time for a meal. Together they all went up to a shed that served as a cantina. The owner had some bottled drinks in an ice-chest and a charcoal brazier with hot coals. Ben asked what he cooked on them and learned the village specialty was shish-kebab. To thank them for facing the dangers of the trip with him, Ben ordered them each a soft drink and shish-kebab on bread. They ate and drank enthusiastically, since the common food of a traveler would normally have been rice with tomato sauce washed down with water.

Ben felt good about the meal. He was acting as a generous host, which his fellow travelers appreciated in traditional style, even though he was the one soliciting their services. He thought of himself as the mutual work team member who asks his age group to clear land with him and then celebrates with a common meal. Or the Chief who collects taxes for his own upkeep, then redistributes part of them in an annual festival to demonstrate the unity of the village.

Ben was not repaying them for their services as an employer pays a worker. Within Miserian tradition, wage labor was a sign of inferiority. Money defined an unequal relationship. He was sharing in response to their sharing with him. Though the relationship between Ben, a big one, and the travelers, little ones, was unequal, gifts softened the impact of inequality.

They returned merrily to the canoe to finish the trip. The boat proceeded through a succession of clearings. At each village Ben asked about specialties it traded. One village provided fresh pineapples, another smoked antelope meat, and a third gathered a bark medicine for intestinal worms.

Were prices fixed by custom? They were, but the buyer still bargained to receive the fixed price. If the product was not in season, did the price change? Of course. Who fixed the price? The market association fixed it. Would the sellers get greedy about their price? No, customers would complain to the Chief, who would intervene. Did sellers give credit? No, that leads to disputes. If there are disputes about quality, who settles them? Each market has a committee of elders who meet to settle disputes. Does anyone give loans to people? Yes, relatives and friends give loans. Does that lead to disputes? Of course, but the disputes would be settled in the clan or community.

The noon sun was hot. Gradually passengers lost interest

in conversation and drifted off to sleep. Forest disappeared, replaced by marsh. The creek widened into a large lagoon with small waves whipped by the ocean breeze. The water smelled different from before. Ben asked about it. Here the tide brought in salt water.

Sunlight danced on the waves. The horizon shimmered. They could see yellow sand dunes now above the green grass. Eventually they spotted the break in the sandbar that led out to the ocean. On the opposite spit of sand appeared a town with low buildings on the horizon. A concrete wharf jutted into the lagoon. The canoeman verified it was the dock for the ferry to the capital. Behind it came two-story cement buildings with storage and shops under the proprietor's apartment. Next, they could see the traditional market with open stalls covered by rusting tin roofs. Beyond it were traditional mud-brick houses.

The town of Sodu represented the economy of Miseria. The market collected local produce brought by canoes from the interior. This produce was exchanged for foreign goods from the import-export businesses, which were resupplied from overseas. Those people closest to the foreigners lived in material comfort; those furthest lived in African tradition.

"Where do the smugglers operate from?" asked Ben.

"They trade in Sodu and keep their boats in fishing villages around the lagoon."

"How do they contact the ships?"

"They use the newspaper or telephone to learn when their ship will moor off the capital. At night they travel to the ship and trade and return before daybreak."

"How many hours does it take to ride to the capital?

"Four."

"When is the next ferry?"

"At sixteen hundred hours."

They arrived in Sodu in the early afternoon. The canoeman guided the boat to a landing near the public market, like the one in Hudu. All was quiet while the merchants took midday siestas in their stalls near their merchandise. The passengers and canoeman disembarked, leaving the youth to guard the boat. Ben asked the canoeman the fare and learned that with thirty bars he could pay for all of the riders.

Standing in the hot sun, Ben said farewell to the other travelers. "I must leave you here," he said regretfully.

His statement caused consternation among them.

Fidel translated, "Papa Salvador said, 'Watch you. Keep you safe.' "

Ben wondered how he could remain invisible to the authorities with a small family and hulking canoeman following him everywhere. Then he suggested, "Can you help me?"

"Fine," came the reply.

"How long does the ferry stay until it returns to the capital?"

"A short time," replied the canoeman.

"I want to go to a cantina near the ferry. You stay there while I buy some European clothes to disguise myself. Then you boys come to tell me when the ferry arrives. The canoeman and I will go to Traficant's store. Do you know where it is?"

"Of course, in town."

"While I talk to Traficant, the family will stay on the ferry to keep it here. Tell the driver, 'A Big Man is coming.' "

They nodded.

"I will come back to the ferry before it leaves. And canoeman will return to his boat. Can the canoeman go back to the village tonight?" asked Ben, realizing the trip coming took almost seven hours.

"I go to friend in the lagoon. At night too many smugglers travel."

At least he would be out of town after they confronted Traficant.

They walked through the sleepy town toward the ferry.

On the way the travelers pointed out Traficant's store and a clothing shop named Chic Image closed during the siesta. Ben also noticed that, if his plan failed, the police station was there. Across from the quay where the ferry from the capital docked, a small restaurant played Afro-Cuban rhythms. They entered, and Ben ordered them all soft drinks and fried bean cakes. The boys ran to the ferry dock and verified that the boat would arrive at 3:30 and leave at 4:00. Ben gave the father money to buy ferry tickets for all of them. He warned them that he would sit separated from them on the way to the capital, but they should watch him in case he needed help.

Ben took Fidel with him back to the clothing store. He told Fidel to return to the canoeman when Ben had bought a full change of clothes.

The proprietor of Chic Image had just opened the metal shutters when Ben arrived dressed as a grubby peasant. Ben politely requested, "Please show a linen suit."

"Do you have eight hundred bars?" he answered gruffly.

Rejoicing in his disguise Ben replied imperiously, "I wish to buy a suit, shirt, shoes, and a hat. If you will not sell, I shall order from Europe."

"Please, let me show you my European clothing."

"Thank you." Ben chose a white shirt so sheer his skin shone through it. The linen suit was loose, yet stylish. He picked out brown oxford shoes, tan socks, and a beautiful panama hat. The total came to 1,450 bars. The proprietor was happy with the sale. Ben bargained for gifts of a Thai silk cravat and two Italian wrap-around sunglasses for the price of one. The proprietor gave him a silvery plastic bag to put his old clothes and files in.

Ben's appearance impressed Fidel, who ran back to tell the others. Ben walked back toward the ferry where the family could see him and then entered an air-conditioned café. He ordered an espresso imperiously, practicing the role he was about to play. From the front window he could see the quay.

He read the *Daily Flag* to get the shipping news. He noticed that a ship, *Tokyo Maru,* had moored to load tropical hardwoods. It would leave for Nigeria in the morning. When the ferry arrived shortly after 3:30, he paid for his coffee and left, motioning to the canoeman to join him. As they walked toward Traficant's store Ben gave him Italian sunglasses. He loved them, and they made him look like a gangster.

Ben left the canoeman outside Traficant's and sauntered in. He spotted the proprietor in the back and cornered him. He chose for himself a name that combined that of his roommate in college and the identity card Manga had lent him. "Hello," he began. "I'm Ebeneezer Abobo. I'd like to make a deal with you."

Traficant froze. "What do you want?" he growled. Apparently he knew Abobo, the jailed con man.

Ben felt exhilaration surging. "How much fly ash do you still have?"

Traficant's eyes shifted nervously to the door, where he saw the canoeman standing. He began to move toward his cash register.

Ben put his silvery bag on the counter and tapped the fingernail file case that protruded from the top. He hoped Traficant was a fan of cowboy movies. "Don't try anything and you'll be fine. I said, 'How much fly ash do you have?' "

Traficant stopped. "Eighteen barrels."

"Deliver them by 3:00 A.M. to the *Tokyo Maru* at the capital and I will forget about how you crossed my brother."

Traficant looked cheated. "I could sell them once the police leave the market."

"I'll save you the trouble. And let you off the shame you brought to my family. Just be there by three!"

"All right."

"I will walk out of here. Don't cause me any trouble and my family will not cause you any trouble. Understand?"

Carrying the bag in his left hand, so he could easily reach

into it with his right, Ben moved sideways out of the store and nodded to the canoeman. They walked back to the ferry on opposite sides of the street, glancing around frequently to ensure they were not being followed.

When they returned, the ferry was filled. Ben saw some police there and wondered if Traficant had raised the alarm. They harassed some illegal peddlers and marched them back to town. Ben handed the canoeman a tip of thirty bars and advised him to put the sunglasses in his pocket, take back streets to his canoe, and leave immediately. They shook hands.

Ben marched on board just as the ferry whistled. He looked back to see if the canoeman followed instructions. The crew cast off shortly and the ferry pulled away. Sodu appeared peaceful as the boat turned and headed through the channel out to sea.

Ben found a seat near a door in the rear lounge of the ferry. He kept his hat and sunglasses on to avoid being identified. The family of Salvador's cousin sat with other passengers on benches with their packages at their feet. Several tried to talk to Ben, who answered with a Nigerian accent, "I no speak Spanish." Peddlers circulated freely; apparently the police raid did not deter them. When they approached Ben, he told them curtly, "Go away."

Eventually everyone's attention was taken by a handsome young man who addressed them. "Ladies and gentlemen. Please excuse me for interrupting you to tell you of the most amazing medical discovery, the magic black stone. Let me tell you about this magic black stone. It will cure skin diseases, wounds, and even snakebites! It draws out the poison from your skin and heals it quickly! All you have to do for skin diseases is to hold the black stone in a gloved hand and rub the skin carefully. You will feel cool as the stone works to remove the disease. For a wound, place the black stone directly on it. It will stick to the wound and stay until the bleeding stops, then it falls off by itself. For snakebites make an inci-

sion between the fang marks and place the black stone there.
The stone will draw out the poison immediately. You will see
it turn white!"

The man continued, "You may ask what such a valuable
black stone costs you! The small stone like this costs four bars
and the large one like that costs five. You may ask why spend
money on a stone you can use only once! But this stone you
can use many times over! After it cures you, just put it in
a pot of boiling water to remove the poison and restore its
original magical powers. Carry it with you on your journey.
Give another to your family. Do I have any customers?" He
looked around.

Ben was fascinated by his mixture of traditional medicine
and modern marketing technique. He found himself wishing
to buy the stone just to examine it for himself.

Other passengers shifted indecisively in their seats. The
man eyed the crowd confidently. "These black stones were
originally found by the Holy Fathers on a mountain in the
north. They used the black stones in their healing ministry,
but did not try to bring them to you people on the coast. Fortunately, I learned their secret and have brought these stones
from far away for your benefit. Remember these stones will
heal skin disease, wounds, and snakebites for only four or five
bars. Who would like one now?"

A young man came forward expectantly. Ben judged he
had been planted in the crowd. Men began to fumble in their
pockets for bills. Women unwrapped their wallets to find
money. Soon a small group of people converged on the man
to buy black stones. Ben estimated the man sold ten stones
right there.

He noticed the man was about his size and rather con-
ceited. In the medicine business a man would believe in magic
or in luck. He did not wear the clothes of a Big Man, though
he might expect that he merited them.

Ben assumed Traficant knew he was on the ferry to the

capital. The smuggling business would not work well without informers. When the ferry docked someone would look for the Big Man in the European suit and panama hat. Ben would try to make sure that Big Man was not himself.

Some dolphins began to follow the boat. A crowd collected along the railings to watch them cavort in the waves. Ben noticed no one was using the latrine. He slipped in and locked the door. The air smelled terrible. He hung his silvery bag on a hook. He slipped off his clothes carefully to avoid dirtying them and put them in the bag. He then put on the dirty village outfit. He remembered to remove the sunglasses and hat. Then he wrapped the bag in his old bandana and tied his files together with the new cravat. He left the latrine relieved to breathe sea air again.

He made his way back to the family, who greeted him familiarly. They traded conversation during the rest of the trip. Ben kept track of the man with the black stones as he worked the decks on his business. When the capital came in sight, he handed the bandana to Fidel. "Go to the man selling black stones. Take out the bag and hand it to him. 'Tell him that the Big Man is grateful for his cure and gives him this gift.' "

The family was perplexed by Ben's proposal.

"Go now," he ordered "and do what I ask."

Fidel left them and returned to announce, "I did it."

"What did the stone seller say?"

" 'Who gave this?' I said, 'A Big Man thanks you.' "

"What did he do?"

"He left and went down below."

Soon Ben saw him strutting proudly in the suit and the Italian sunglasses. Ben could see police taking positions on the dock for the ferry's arrival.

Though Ben realized that he should separate from the family, he wanted them not to think he would dump them because he arrived in the capital. He distributed to the boys some candy he had bought for them at the café in Sodu. After transferring his files into the bandana, he gave the cravat to the mother. He gave Pedro the panama hat as a present, telling him to pack it until they returned home. He then handed him an envelope for Salvador with five hundred-bar bills and a note wishing him well. The rest of his money was hidden in his underwear, very uncomfortably. He hoped these precautions would permit him to reach dry land.

Ben and the family joined the crowd and the exit. The police blocked their way, checking passengers' identities as they disembarked. Ben held back, allowing others to surge past him. He could see Corporal Sodunu behind them overseeing the operation. Eventually a policeman spotted the Big Man in the stern. He shouted for support and plunged through the crowd followed by two others. Sodunu walked to the edge of the dock to identify his suspect. The crowd surged off the ferry with Ben in it. He hurried past the family toward the public transportation. Behind him he could hear an argument between the police and the medicine seller.

Ben walked past the nearest taxis, which were boxed in by the crowd. He hailed one in the street. "Take me to the National University."

The driver looked at him disapprovingly and stated, "Take the bus."

Ben pulled out ten bars and challenged him. "You get all of this if I arrive within ten minutes." With no further argument from the driver, Ben jumped in.

The taxi screeched through a U-turn and sped off. Ben could see policemen running off the ferry shouting to others in the street. His taxi turned the corner safely and the scene disappeared.

The driver eyed him suspiciously in the rearview mirror. "Someone looks for you?"

Ben tried to look impatient. "I am in a hurry to see my friend. I cannot wait for roadblocks."

"Roadblock at the university main gate."

"I am going to senior faculty housing."

"Fine. I drop you at faculty gate."

Ben was back in the rush-rush of the city again. They arrived quickly at the faculty gate. He paid the taxi driver and walked past the guard. Soon he found the Gomez bungalow and knocked.

Señora Gomez appeared in an evening gown and opened the door. "Dr. Mchunguzi, we worried about you."

"I'm okay. Is your husband in?"

"He is at the hotel for the Prime Minister's speech. Come in. I don't want you to be recognized."

He entered, but hesitated to sit down in his dirty clothes. He felt like a village relative in a city home.

"Please come into the kitchen where you cannot be seen. What can I get you after your journey?"

"Some water, please. I just came from Sodu. The trader Traficant is involved in the toxic waste trade."

She made a sandwich for him too. "Widow Hudunu told us her husband had found out about toxic waste just before he was murdered."

"Then the remaining clue is who took the swim trunks from the front desk and put them on Hudunu and why."

"The swim trunks — nobody has spoken of them. I suppose the murderer wanted to conceal the body on the beach until he or she escaped."

Ben became pensive. "Or tried to implicate someone else in the murder. Me, for instance."

"But you were not here yet!" She looked hard at him.

"I would have arrived before the murder was discovered."

"I doubt it. We have a coroner in Miseria. He determined that the death occurred during the night. So you were not implicated."

He was relieved that she trusted him. "Would you ask your husband to find out who took the swim trunks from the front desk? We would then know one of the accomplices."

"Could you come with me to the reception? You could clear your name in front of everyone."

"Corporal Sodunu has the police chasing me. I do not know if Cristobal Mulama is involved too."

"After he heard about the raid on the village, my husband asked Mulama for an explanation. He claimed the raid had nothing to do with his investigation of the Hudunu case. It was designed to catch smugglers."

Ben was perplexed. "The police came into the room where I hid and demanded that my hosts give up 'the alien.' Would they refer to a smuggler that way?"

"My husband asked specifically if he was looking for you, and Mulama declared that he had given no orders to find you. As if he did not care, he did not question my husband further on that matter."

"Have I been named on the radio as a fugitive?"

"I do not believe so."

"If Sodunu or Mulama were looking for me and caught me, what would they do to me?"

"They might take you to a detention camp and force you to confess to the murder. Unfortunately, they might succeed."

"But you said the coroner's report indicated the death occurred before my arrival in the country. Furthermore, I have a witness that I did not leave the airport until after the body was discovered."

"Both the coroner and the airport inspector must do what the government wishes."

"Earlier you offered to take me to the reception. That would be a risk for you and me. Do you still recommend it?"

"I don't know. If you confront Mulama publicly with your explanation of the murder, he cannot accuse you at all. If my husband talks privately, he can always deny the conversation after you reappear. If you stay here, you are at risk too. They have come several times already to question us."

"So you believe the trip is worth the risk? Sodunu's police are looking for me in the city right now."

"Teresa and her husband are driving me to the reception, so there are other witnesses involved. The police will still have roadblocks and could pull you out of the car, unless we could disguise you. You don't look much like my husband, though. Can you drive well?"

"Of course."

"The police would not know our chauffeur is off this evening. Do you think you could act the part?"

"I shall try."

"Good. I will call Teresa. Please clean up and change clothes quickly."

Ben showered gratefully. The soap gave him a sense of relief from the mosquito bites. He dressed in the university driver uniform.

As he went out the back door with the car keys, he realized he would be driving on the right side of the road. He warmed up the motor for a long time while he inspected the dashboard and worked the gearshift carefully. Then he gingerly drove around to the front door to meet Señora Gomez.

The next obstacle was the locked front gate. Fortunately, a house servant appeared to let them out. The *señora* gave him directions. He negotiated the right turn carefully to keep from switching sides of the road. At the main gate to the National University a bored policeman recognized the car and waved them through.

During the ride Señora Gomez made him memorize directions to the hotel. Without introducing Ben, she greeted Teresa and her husband, who sat in the front seat beside Ben. It would be more natural for them to be ignorant of Ben's identity.

As they approached the commercial district a police officer stopped them. Ben feared the officer might address him in a Miserian language. Seeing the formally dressed group, he

demanded in Spanish to see the car documents and the identity card of Teresa's husband. Ben knew the car papers were
in the glove compartment, so he nodded and presented them.
Finding nothing wrong the policeman waved them past.

"I have the power of the Trickster," thought Ben.

They arrived at the Grand Hotel and Ben stopped at the
main entrance. As he opened the door for Teresa, she whispered to him, "Thank you, Ben." Señora Gomez instructed
him publicly to park the car and return with some files. He
found a parking place in back. Other drivers were joking together under a street light. He tried to look very preoccupied
with his files. They called to him in the vernacular language.
He smiled, waved, and turned the corner quickly.

Though police and security agents were standing guard he
had no difficulty entering the hotel lobby in his uniform. He
joined Señora Gomez and Teresa, who were waiting for him
there. He could see the student aides helping to clear chairs
from the ballroom after the Prime Minister's speech in preparation for the dance. Rosa was overseeing the conference
cocktail party in an adjoining room.

Señora Gomez spotted her husband and directed them in.
At the door a hotel employee stopped Ben, who protested that
he was only bringing files in for the conference. Nevertheless,
he had to wait until Dean Gomez came and invited him into
the room. Ben handed him the files.

"Why did you come here?" asked Gomez surprised.

"I learned Traficant is in the toxic waste business. I made
an appointment with his relative in Sodu to deliver a shipment
of the waste to a ship tonight. We need police cooperation to
catch him in the act. I also know that the person who took
the swim trunks from the front desk was involved with the
murder."

"Everyone is here, except the Prime Minister, who left
right after his speech. We could ask Mulama to take over."

"Is he involved?"

"Even so, half the government cabinet is in this crowd. He will have to catch the murderer once the evidence becomes public."

As he talked with Dean Gomez, he noticed the crowd looking at him peculiarly. Many of the conference delegates were his friends, even though their last meeting was long enough ago that they had trouble recognizing him. Mulama had spotted him, though. It was time to act.

Dean Gomez took the microphone. "I have an important announcement. We have all missed the presence of Dr. Mchunguzi Maluum, the organizer of this conference, just as we regretted the absence of a dear colleague, Dr. Xavier Hudunu. As I told you earlier, Dr. Mchunguzi had to take an unforeseen trip to check some matters related to the conference. I am happy to announce that he has returned." Applause greeted the news.

Gomez continued, "At the time of his death Dr. Hudunu was investigating the importation of toxic waste into Miseria." The crowd became very still. "I will let Dr. Mchunguzi explain what he has found."

The crowd gasped as he handed the microphone to Ben. "Thank you, my friends, colleagues, and distinguished visitors. I must explain that I have been in disguise while I made an investigation of smuggling. Today I visited the city of Sodu and confronted the proprietor of Traficant Import-Export there. He acknowledged that he still has eighteen barrels of toxic waste and agreed to deliver them by boat to the *Tokyo Maru* by 3:00 A.M. I am sure that Inspector Mulama will deal with that smuggler with all the rigor that Miserian law prescribes."

Mulama stepped forward. His eyes shifted quickly as he stood before his political patrons. He announced, "I will organize the investigation immediately."

"In addition," Ben interjected, "I learned an important

clue to the murder of Xavier Hudunu. Would the doorman please call in the desk clerk!"

The clerk arrived looking very frightened.

Ben looked sternly at him. "I am Dr. Mchunguzi, organizer of this conference."

"Yes, sir."

"Tell me who took the swim trunks from the front desk last Friday night that were found later on Dr. Hudunu's body."

The clerk hesitated, his eyes glancing around the faces in the room. He saw the hotel director, Musa, who nodded to him. "Señor Traficant of the import shop in the commercial district took the swim trunks."

Ben's heart leapt. "Thank you. You may go. Inspector Mulama, what needs to be done?" He felt triumphant.

Though Mulama looked angry, he answered resolutely. "Dr. Mchunguzi, I shall arrest both the Traficant brothers this evening." He left the room and called for his men.

Dean Gomez hugged Ben. The crowd surged forward to greet him. He shook hands and exchanged good wishes with his friends. Politicians waited for the news reporters to set up their cameras. Then they asked him to change into suitable attire for photos. Said one, "The Prime Minister will be disappointed he missed your arrival."

Dean Gomez took him up to the Royalty Suite to change into his suit. "I would have advised you to let me arrange with Mulama to arrest the Traficant brothers. You took a big risk that the police would catch you first."

"I know that, but I wanted to force Mulama to solve the case by publicly shaming him."

"Do you think he knew Traficant was involved?"

"I don't know. Do you?"

"He might have."

"He did not ask about the swim trunks. Was he deliberately avoiding that clue?"

"Traficant was too small a businessman for Mulama to cooperate with him."

"So you believe I took the risk needlessly. I also risked the people who had helped me."

"I am happy you were successful, my friend."

"Perhaps I wanted too much to come back and participate in this conference."

"We are all happy about that."

They returned to the impromptu news conference in the ballroom. Ben shook hands with government Ministers in front of the cameras and then was ushered to the table prepared for him. Dean Gomez sat with Ben before the microphones of the Miserian National Radio and Television, Nigerian Broadcasting, Radio Cameroon, and Spanish International Radio. The guests all gathered at the back of the room to observe.

The first question was, "What led you to suspect the Traficant brothers?"

Ben replied, "I learned about the illegal trade in toxic waste by touring local markets with economics professors and students from the National University. A chemistry professor at the National University confirmed that the white stones were harmful. Other Miserians suggested to me that the Traficant brothers operated out of Sodu, where they would have excellent smuggling contacts to bring in toxic waste and distribute it. So I went to Sodu posing as a foreign businessman wishing to buy toxic waste, and Traficant agreed to sell it and deliver it tonight. When I knew he was guilty, I reported to Miserian authorities, who have taken the matter in hand."

Ben had not thought about his answers. He tried to praise his friends at the National University, which he knew would gratify Dean Gomez, and avoid criticizing officials, who might still cause trouble for his conference.

The next question could have been, "Why did you not

contact the police in Sodu?" Instead, a reporter asked, "Were you in danger contacting those ruthless smugglers?"

He was relieved that the journalists did not ask very probing questions. "No, I disguised myself to avoid recognition." He did not need to add anything about the power of the Trickster.

"What is your impression of Miseria?"

He had rehearsed this answer. "I have visited Miseria several times, and I am impressed with the efforts of its people to overcome underdevelopment. I proposed that we hold our World Economics Association conference here in order to make contact with your National University and to encourage your efforts to develop the national economy."

Mulama entered looking very pleased with himself. He surveyed the room and then walked up to the microphones beside Ben. The representative of the Miserian National Radio and Television obliged him with a question. "Do we have any report on your investigations, Inspector Mulama?"

"Yes, I am happy to announce that in Sodu our units intercepted the smuggler Traficant with eighteen barrels of toxic waste in his boat. A raid on his warehouse produced an additional twenty barrels. He and two accomplices have been detained for questioning. In the capital we have learned that his brother fled at approximately five o'clock with his family and all documents and cash. He chartered a boat to escape. We have mounted a search by air, land, and sea for him. Any Miserian seeing suspicious movements should contact immediately the appropriate authorities! Our government has appealed to governments of neighboring African countries to arrest and return this international agent of foreign poison."

Ben could see Mulama had a great future in politics.

Mulama then turned to Ben and declared, "All Miserians owe a debt of gratitude to Dr. Mchunguzi of Kenya, who in a spirit of unselfish African solidarity risked his life to discover the source of toxic waste in our nation!" He then led applause as the camera turned toward the back of the room to record the elite's appreciation of Ben. Ben shook Mulama's hand and said for the microphones, "Thank you, inspector." Pleased with themselves, they exchanged pleasantries. With that the news conference ended.

Dean Gomez looked hard at Mulama and stated, "Corporal Sodunu helped cover up the smuggling by Traficant."

"We know. He is in detention as well as three members of his family. He must answer not only as an accomplice in smuggling but also for his lawless raid on your family's village. The police will hold discipline hearings on him this week."

"Thank you." They shook hands.

Musa proposed a toast for Ben. "To the man who saved us from the scourge of toxic waste!"

"And revealed the murderer of Hudunu!" added Rosa.

The crowd advanced back to greet him. He shook hands with the well-wishers. Dossou and Zande clapped him on the back. Teresa shook his hand and introduced him to her husband, a leading pharmacist.

"I apologize for putting you and your wife through the risk of traveling with a wanted man."

"Don't worry. We could have pleaded ignorance," he answered.

Ben avoided looking at Teresa.

Victor Vodumanyon pumped his hand. "Until tonight my colleagues shunned me, accusing me of selling out to foreign toxic waste merchants. Now they all tell me that government controlled disposal is preferable to illegal activities."

"Does your name have anything to do with the Trickster?" Ben asked.

"Yes, it means 'Vodu not good.' The Trickster is one of the Vodu Spirits."

"Tonight the Trickster may have helped you."

Chapter VI

The Power of the Trickster

☙

S IX DAYS LATER Ben stood before the assembled conference to deliver his final speech. He was relieved at having
had the time to prepare his remarks for the conference, since
he still had to be careful with his statements. Seated with him
on the platform were the Ministers of the Interior, Agriculture, Education, and Foreign Trade. The former Minister of
Foreign Trade, who came from Sodu, had been implicated in
the smuggling of toxic waste and arrested. His successor was
the former Minister of Education. A surprise appointment,
a professor from the Teachers College became the new Minister of Education despite her lack of political backing. Her
colleagues at the National University were delighted to see
her competence recognized.

"Your Excellencies the Minister of the Interior, the Minister of Agriculture, the Minister of Foreign Trade, and the
Minister of Education, academic colleagues from Miseria and
abroad, Ladies and Gentlemen,

"I am delighted to address you this evening at the conclu-
sion of the World Economics Association Regional Conference in Miseria. Speaking for the conference, we are grateful

to the nation of Miseria for its wonderful hospitality. My friends, you outdo yourselves in African hospitality!"

Applause from the foreigners. It was true! Rosa had done a marvelous job of catering, well worth the money she had extracted from him. The village cotton cooperative that they visited had greeted them dressed in their best clothes and singing lustily.

"We are also grateful that the Miserian justice system has caught those responsible for smuggling and is pursuing the murderer of our beloved friend and colleague, Dr. Xavier Hudunu."

Ben turned and nodded to the Minister of the Interior, who accepted the praise with evident satisfaction. Ben proceeded in order of political prominence.

"We have had ample opportunities during visits at the Cotton Cooperative of Mamu and at the Rice Project of Dota to observe the development efforts of the Miserian people and its government." He nodded to the Minister of Agriculture.

"We are pleased to thank the newly appointed Minister of Foreign Trade for the help he gave in organizing this conference, when he served in the Ministry of Education. We wish him well in his new responsibilities."

The Minister of Foreign Trade smiled and waved to his friends in the audience as they clapped for him.

"We are also delighted to learn of the appointment of our colleague as the new Minister of Education."

Spontaneous applause caused her to smile and wave in response.

"Often in Africa a professional group at the end of a conference presents official resolutions. This is not the practice of the World Economics Association, nor could we agree on such resolutions. We represent a broad variety of perspectives on economic theory. We believe in the free debate of ideas in order to arrive at truth.

"However, on the issue of the freedom of our members,

to state responsibly their professional opinions the World Economics Association is adamant. For this reason we have addressed three 'Open Letters' to governments in Africa that have jailed or harassed economists."

The politicians were very quiet, lest he mention any names of governments that might embarrass them.

Ben summarized the highlights of the conference, "First, our conference examined the reduction of tropical forest in Africa at 6 percent per year until only 2.5 million square miles remain. We recognized that historically conservation of forests has been a hotly debated political issue in Africa because colonial governments claimed common lands that villages allocated traditionally. The colonialists excluded the African villagers from hunting, gathering, and firewood collection that were essential to their way of life. So the people were forced to sell their agricultural products or find wage employment. At the same time we affirm that Africa's tropical forests are an international asset producing valuable benefits for which our countries and our populations should be reimbursed. We, therefore, claim that industrial countries should reimburse our countries for the global services of carbon dioxide reduction and pollution abatement performed by our tropical rain forests. These payments would not be foreign aid, but reimbursements for services rendered!"

Applause greeted this statement.

"These payments can serve partly to improve management of tropical forest resources. At the same time traditional villagers should be reimbursed for the added cost to them of intensifying agricultural production. If they no longer have extra land that can be left fallow to reconstitute its fertility, they must be able to afford to apply organic and chemical fertilizers and to cultivate more carefully. This implies provision of effective technical advice."

Ben could see the growing tension in the Minister of Agriculture's face.

"In other words, payments from the beneficiaries of the global biosphere reserve must be transferred to the farmers in return for giving up their traditional rights to the forest.

"In addition, our conference considered sustainable development of our national economies. We must develop indigenous appropriate technology, which are techniques that use locally available resources and do not harm the ecosystem. We heard reports on several new discoveries that could greatly benefit African societies.

"The first is intercropping whereby hedges ten yards apart in fields provide the farmer with firewood, animal fodder, and compost while also improving the land by preventing wind and water erosion, by protecting it from the sun's heat, and by providing nitrogen from the roots directly to the soil.

"Secondly, new biotechnologies have finally reached tropical food plants, such as yams and cassava, which now increase yields and resist diseases. We anticipate progress in African agriculture similar to the Green Revolutions in wheat and rice production in other parts of the world!"

Ben noticed the Minister of Agriculture taking careful notes.

"The third one is fish farming. Fish can be grown in ponds built to store water for the dry season. Fish farms can also be built in the middle of shallow lagoons by placing stakes close enough together for small fish to enter but large fish to remain trapped. The fisherman supplies fodder to this artificially fenced fish farm to attract more fish. Once they grow, fishermen extend their nets around the field, remove the sticks and harvest all the fish. Finally, we discussed the use of solar energy for drying rural produce, pumping water, and providing electricity to dispersed areas.

"We concluded that the difficulty is not with finding appropriate technologies but with developing means of dissemination in societies with low levels of literacy and traditional outlooks.

"Our conference also discussed the important issue of the structural adjustment programs (SAPs) negotiated by the International Monetary Fund with African governments. It noted that the emphasis on lowering the value of the national currency compared to foreign currencies made imports more expensive. When these imports consist of food, spare parts, and medicines, the effects of higher prices on the population are most serious. At the same time government spending is cut to balance the budget. The effects of these SAPs fall hardest on the poor, as social programs in education, health, and social welfare are the first to be cut."

Ben heard the voice of the Minister of Education saying, "Yes, Yes."

He continued, "Let us remember the international context in which the debt crisis occurred. The industrial countries, afraid because the prices of raw materials were mounting faster than the growth rate of their economies, engineered tight money growth policies that raised interest rates and cut raw material prices. The developing countries that had borrowed when credit was plentiful at low interest rates must pay high interest rates to service their debts while receiving reduced prices for their raw material exports. Developing countries are paying much of the price for the anti-inflation policies enforced by industrial countries.

"At the moment we in Africa are paying back more in reimbursement than we receive in foreign aid. The poor of the world are subsidizing the rich, because the rich chose to raise their interest rates."

Applause broke out, led by the African elite who saw their future mortgaged by the heavy debts their countries had incurred.

"Finally, I would like to pay tribute to Dr. Xavier Hudunu's contribution to African economics, of which I became more aware as I researched his murder."

At this the audience became respectfully silent.

"His method was always to start with actual examples of men and women whose businesses provide valuable goods and services and to ask what are the limits for expansion of these businesses. We have seen examples of thriving women traders in the markets of Miseria, of a developing entertainment business, and of production of agricultural implements appropriate to the soil, farming styles, and repair capacities of rural areas. Clearly, entrepreneurs exist, but how can they expand and create prosperity for our people?

"Dr. Hudunu showed that all too often the limits are managerial ability. Since owners trust only themselves or family members to manage, they will not hire managers to expand their businesses. Furthermore, the systems of control through accounting and audits are not secure and the courts do not protect business owners. Dr. Hudunu noted that in traditional African society the systems of control for property are quite secure. The sellers and producers associations do not mismanage goods credited to them, and they discipline members who put self-interest above the good name of the association. So why do we fail to trust them in modern businesses?

"Dr. Hudunu believed that prosperity came from labor and the fruits of prosperity should go to those who labor. I often discussed with him his belief that God created this world through labor and therefore sanctified creative labor even though human beings were condemned to labor after their expulsion from the Garden of Eden!"

Ben knew he needed all of God's and Hudunu's authority to get through the next part.

"He believed in divine law. Therefore he believed that those officials and big businesses who cheat the laborer out of his or her due recompense are subject to God's wrath!"

The Minister of the Interior squirmed and Ben wondered if he had crossed the line.

"In particular, Dr. Hudunu criticized smuggling, the smugglers as well as the officials and laws that make it profitable.

He advocated regulations that would make productive businesses more profitable than illegal ones. So it is not surprising that he died at the hands of a smuggler!"

Now the Minister of Foreign Trade looked pained.

Ben now looked at the student aides and their friends standing at the back of the hall. They were smiling.

"Dr. Hudunu had an abiding faith in the youth whom he taught so well. He believed that, if he presented a vision of Miserian society in which each member labored both in self-interest and in the interests of Africa, the college graduates would take up the challenge. That is the legacy he left to us."

"I would like to thank the economists who presented the interesting papers we have studied during the past week, as well as the audience that made these presentations so invigorating. Our duty to challenge each other and to teach our students is our contribution to the future of Africa. May our belief in truth guide us in our vocations as economists."

Applause greeted the end of his speech. He bowed to the government Ministers, who appeared relieved that he had not demanded more of them. He sat down, thinking of all he could have said about the importance of honest and efficient government.

Dean Gomez rose and intoned, "On behalf of the organizing committee we wish to thank the World Economics Association and its regional secretary for their organization of this conference." He led the applause.

Ben rose again and shook hands with his friend.

"And now I declare this conference closed."

Ben turned and shook hands with the new Minister of Foreign Trade, "Congratulations on your new post, Your Excellency."

"Thank you. I hope I can achieve results as positive as I did in inviting you to organize this conference."

"I hope so too. Are you planning to change policies?"

"Yes. For one thing we have lowered the import duties on

consumer electronic parts so that we can assemble them in Miseria."

"That sounds like an excellent idea. Can you export consumer electronics to earn foreign currency too?" Ben thought of the entrepreneurs in Hudu and the traders in Sodu.

"I have begun negotiations with neighboring countries."

"If you could develop film producers, you might be able to preserve and spread Miserian culture."

"We have contacted UNESCO about setting up studios in our country."

"I wish you the best in your endeavors." He turned to the Minister of Education. "Señora, my congratulations."

"Thank you, Dr. Mchunguzi."

"What are your plans now?"

"I have sent notices to our teachers and professors that I will encourage publishing of textbooks adapted to Miseria. From now on they will receive full royalties for their work."

"Dean Gomez will be delighted."

She smiled. "I know. He suggested the idea to me. We have a very knowledgeable intelligentsia in this country, as you have seen, Dr. Mchunguzi."

"I agree. I have been impressed at how they held their own in debates during the conference."

"I believe that if we let them write freely our country will benefit even though they might uncover some more embarrassments for the government."

"You are a brave woman."

"We shall see. I trust my colleagues in education cherish their freedom more than the opportunity to replace me as Minister of Education."

"I hope for your success."

Ben turned to the Minister of the Interior and smiled. "I appreciate the way your police cleaned up the murder of our colleague, Professor Hudunu."

"Thank you, Dr. Mchunguzi. We are ashamed that our officer was involved with the smugglers, but we have punished him and rooted out his influence in our police force."

"It is to your credit that you acted decisively against corruption, Your Excellency." Ben tried not to sound sarcastic.

Other well-wishers interrupted them.

Ben turned to Falco, "Have you resolved the legal problems about your arrival?"

"Yes, that 'fat cat' lawyer got the charges dropped once he got paid."

"Have you filed your flight plan for the return?"

"You bet."

"I wish you a safe journey. Is Piccione accompanying you?"

"He hasn't decided yet."

"Well, good luck."

Ben found the Minister of Agriculture. "I want to thank your staff for arranging visits to the rice project and cotton cooperative. We enjoyed very much the welcome they gave us."

"I hope you found the projects well-run."

"We have several agricultural economists who asked pointed questions. I was impressed that your staff understood all of them and answered them honestly. They seemed ready to accept suggestions and to debate their usefulness."

"I heard that your conference was critical."

"Certainly, economists are supposed to be critical! They admire professionals who can stand up to them."

"Good, I am glad to hear that. I was not sure what impression we made."

"If any of the suggestions I made in my speech are useful to you, I can refer you to the speakers who are experts on the subject."

"Thank you. I took notes and will talk with my staff about your ideas. If you can help us, I will contact you."

Ben wondered why the man was so evasive when he could make direct contacts in the room.

Ben found Rosa. "Señora, I want to thank you for your efforts. I was proud that our visitors received such good treatment."

Rosa smiled modestly. "We did our best with the means we had."

"You did splendidly, Señora."

"Thank you, Dr. Mchunguzi. I enjoyed your conference. The delegates were fun-loving without being obnoxious."

"I am glad to hear that. However, I thought vomiting in the lobby was obnoxious."

"By one person? No, I am pleased when only one person had too much to drink."

"Several delegates have said they wish to return."

"I am glad. One talked to me. Please tell the others to see me before they leave."

"Well, I should say goodbye. I am leaving tonight."

"I hoped you would stay and relax. The room is available."

"No. My wife told me on the telephone that two children are ill. She complains that this happens only when I travel."

"I am sorry. You must make your family first priority."

"Yes," he answered, surprised that she put family first. He shook her hand.

Biggles wandered up to him. "Well, this hotel will be quite dull without your conference."

"I hope you did not mind the noise."

"Not at all. I enjoyed meeting you too."

"Thank you. I enjoyed our conversation on Miserian vernacular languages. I believe your time has been well spent here."

"Yes. I hope to see you back in Britain next year. Cheerio."

Ben saw Teresa and her husband and maneuvered near them. "I want to say goodbye. I leave tonight."

"I am sorry," Teresa replied. "We hoped you would stay."

"My children are ill, and I want to see them."

"Nothing serious, I hope."

"Chicken pox."

Her husband responded professionally. "Be careful. It can lead to complications, though it is more dangerous here than in Europe."

"I know. I don't like them to be ill when I am so far away."

Dossou and Zande came over to them. "So you are leaving immediately?" asked Dossou.

"Tonight."

"The local arrangements committee wants you to come and read the conference evaluation forms."

"I have enjoyed meeting you," Ben said to the couple.

"Please come back and see us," replied Teresa. She and her husband shook hands with him.

Dossou and Zande led him out to the lobby, where they found Dean Gomez and Assistant Minister Asaba. Together they went up to his room to read evaluation forms.

"Can I get you anything?" asked Ben politely.

"No, thank you," answered Asaba.

"Not after the reception downstairs," replied Gomez.

It was evident they had drunk and eaten their fill at the party.

Dossou read some evaluations and concluded with evident relief, "They found the accommodations charming."

"These Europeans love quaint colonial hotels," suggested Zande.

"This person is probably from East Africa. He compares it to a hotel in Nairobi."

Ben laughed. "Don't look at me. I haven't filled one out yet."

"This one disliked driving so far from his hotel to the conference," observed Gomez.

"But he chose to move to the other hotel, knowing he

would have to take taxis back and forth. Sometimes I wonder about the rationality of my fellow economists!" Ben exclaimed.

"They all liked the visits to the development projects," said Asaba.

Gomez added, "I agree. I guess the hospitality charmed them, whether they were Africans or not."

"Or the speeches bored them?" suggested Zande.

Dossou would not let him get away with that statement. "Were you bored? You disagreed with everything. If anybody was bored it was from hearing you say, 'According to dependency theory. . . .' Then when you presented dependency theory, it sounded like a program of substituting local manufacturing for imports and developing a common market. Many other economists propose the same policies."

Gomez interjected, "Please, we must finishing reading these evaluations before our friend's flight."

They both looked disappointed not to continue their favorite debate.

"This person much enjoyed the variety of viewpoints presented by the speakers," observed Ben.

"I have one here who disliked hearing Communists speak," noted Gomez. "None of the East Europeans sounded dogmatic. They were more enthusiastic about free markets than the West Europeans."

Ben tried to sum up the discussion, "I think we have a democratic difference of opinion with the person who is against Communists. We dislike their politics, but we defend their right to speak openly."

"The Prime Minister will be happy to hear that this delegate liked his speech," stated Asaba proudly. "I am happy too. I wrote the first draft for him."

"Congratulations," said Zande, who was not noted for praising politicians. "I was proud to hear that speech too."

"I am sorry I missed it," said Ben.

Gomez observed, "Several have said nice things about you."

"Yes!" added Dossou admiringly.

"Thank you," said Ben.

Asaba looked at Gomez. "They also appreciated your chairing the important sessions."

Ben stretched his arms. "Well, I have read them all and am proud to take them back with me to show the Board of Directors. Unless you would like to show them first to the Prime Minister?" He looked at Asaba.

"I have made notes on the conference for him."

"Good, please give him our thanks for participating," added Ben officiously.

"I brought some four corners to thank the ancestors for watching over us," said Gomez. "Bring some glasses and we will go onto the verandah."

The five of them sat silently while Dean Gomez performed libations. This time in the garden a band played sweet Afro-Cuban rhythms as guests danced and talked quietly. A full moon shone on the sand dune where Hudunu had died. The sea seemed tranquil.

Ben broke the spell. "I wish I could stay and enjoy this with you, but I must check in by eleven."

"I'll drive you," offered Gomez.

"No, I have a car and chauffeur," said Asaba generously.

Ben did not look at his colleague, who undoubtedly was exhausted after the week of intensive meetings. "If the chauffeur is awake, I can go with him."

"We will all come," added Asaba convivially.

They nodded agreement. Ben knew he would feel safer at the airport with a send-off group. He phoned the desk for a steward to take his luggage. They all went down together.

In the lobby they met two student aides from the conference. "Do you have a way to get home?" Ben asked.

"Yes," replied one and added, "We stayed to speak with you."

"I must leave shortly," said Ben doubtfully. He was puzzled, because he had officially thanked them earlier and given them each their present.

The student continued nervously, "We would like scholarships to study in Europe."

"Which year are you?"

"Third year."

"Our association distributes scholarships the final year through a committee of your teachers."

"We are not sure to receive them."

Ben felt irritated. "No one is sure to receive scholarships. The scholarships are distributed according to test results. I cannot help you."

The students slunk off.

Ben glared at Dossou, "Are they your students?"

Dossou sighed, "They are doing badly at the University, but their families expect the world from them. While they worry about their future scholarships, they fail to take advantage of their current scholarships by studying."

The official limousine arrived. Ben paid the two stewards five bars each. He had to spend the money he had reserved for taxi fare, since he could not take it from the country. The stewards were delighted to help him solve his problem.

As the limousine pulled out of the hotel Ben noted, "Traficant's store has already been torn down."

"That is where the new electronics factory will be built," said Asaba.

"Cartagena is losing no time remodeling too, it appears. I guess the competition with Rosa Lugner will now get fierce." Ben turned to Dean Gomez. "Please greet your relatives in the village for me."

"I will. They were very glad that you came to visit on Sunday."

"I wanted to thank them." Ben remained vague, because the others did not know who had hid him for two days. He was not sure if elements of the police might still be loyal to Corporal Sodunu.

He remembered the reception in Francisco Gomez's house. Everyone was glad to see that justice had brought him back to his position of Big Man. He had thanked them for their loving hospitality. They took him to greet the Chief. Again, Ben praised the wonderful village without revealing the names of his benefactors. He did not want the Chief to feel slighted, since he had been kept out of the conspiracy. The Chief gracefully covered his ignorance by accepting the compliments on behalf of the villagers. Ben then visited Salvador briefly, who was delighted to see him. His cousin Pedro arrived with the family. Ben noticed that Salvador had more medicines now and felt good about his gift. In a spirit of open hospitality the villagers invited Ben to return. Ben was grateful for their help.

The limousine sped through familiar city streets, though Ben was surprised to see the lively late-night activity. The car honked at pedestrians returning from the movies. Food peddlers remained open to catch nighttime clientele. Record stores blared their wares into the night.

"Are people safe on the streets at night?" asked Ben.

"Oh, no! Last year someone was robbed here," answered Zande.

"Were they attacked?"

"No, threatened so they would give their wallet."

"Since then has there been other crime?"

"Maybe snatching a peddler's money."

"I wish I lived in such a crime-free environment. They say London is a civilized city where the police don't carry guns, but there is a crime each week in my neighborhood. I shall miss Africa."

"When are you coming back?" asked Gomez.

"Soon, I hope. I am taking my family home for a visit to

Kenya for the Christmas holidays. When my contract expires the following June, I hope to return to teaching."

"Would you be interested in coming as a visiting professor to Miseria?" Gomez continued.

"I would be flattered at such an offer. The difficulty is in educating my children in a different school system."

"Our university would be happy to invite you. Maybe for a semester? So it does not interfere with their education during a whole year."

"Thank you. I have a lot of friends here."

The limousine arrived at the airport, and everyone got out. Ben was grateful that the official car gave him immunity from any harassment by officials. He called the chauffeur and gave him a ten-bar tip he had reserved for the taxi. It pleased the man immensely.

Asaba marched Ben to the front of the check-in line. Ben knew the European tourists were angry that a Miserian politician pushed ahead of them. He knew, though, that if he stood in line, his entourage would have to wait with him.

The airline personnel treated him with due respect. He noted with approval that they inspected his bags thoroughly and pulled the batteries from his transistor radio as a safety measure against bombs. They also asked him whether he received any gifts lest he inadvertently carry a parcel bomb. He felt safe with their professionalism.

When he had finished paying his airport tax, Dean Gomez brought the group together to deliver a prayer for his journey. "Oh, God, watch over our brother, Dr. Mchunguzi. Bring him safely home to his family, who needs him. May he return soon among us. Amen."

They waved to him as he entered the doors of the security cubicles. The security check brought back the feelings he had on arrival. He was alone in the room with two Customs inspectors. One took his declaration of foreign currency and asked, "How much Miserian money are you carrying?"

"Seven bars," replied Ben, knowing the limit was ten.

"Show them to me."

Ben brought out seven bars and change.

"Show me your foreign currency and travelers checks."

Ben pulled out his money belt and watched him expertly count the money. The totals added up exactly to his accounts. At the same time the other officer patted him down to make sure nothing else was in his pockets. He found a British ten-penny piece.

"Show me the receipts for exchange."

Ben handed them and the officer examined carefully the official stamps on each.

The officer seemed disappointed that all was in order. "All right, you may go."

Ben stuffed the money and receipts back in his pockets and asked, "Is Chief Inspector De Almeida on duty tonight?"

The officers stiffened. One took him through a door into De Almeida's office.

De Almeida greeted him with a smile and a handshake. "Professor Mchunguzi, a pleasure to see you again."

"Likewise," responded Ben.

"Is anything wrong?"

"Not at all. I just wanted to say goodbye to you."

The Customs officer was obviously relieved and left.

"I am pleased you came to see me. As you can see, I work all hours and sometimes have free time. Can I order you something?"

"No, thank you. I just had something when the local arrangements committee sent me off."

"I hope you had a good conference."

"We did. Your son performed wonderfully."

"I am glad."

"Yes. He asked to run errands in the main meeting room, so he could listen to the conference. From the questions he asked the delegates I believe he learned a great deal."

"Wonderful. I have always told him to learn as much as possible."

"He also helped me very much."

"Really?"

"A delegate was harassing another professor's wife one evening. And your son walked up to him and started asking about his own family. The man burst into tears and your son spent the next hour listening to his lonely life story. The woman slipped away without her husband knowing about the incident. Your son was an excellent diplomat. Like his father!"

"Wonderful. My son told me about the incident but did not brag about his own contribution."

"Well, I wanted to thank you for helping free me of suspicion of murder. I think Sodunu might have tried to frame me had you not spoken up."

"It is my duty to speak the truth!"

"I am grateful you do your duty, Chief Inspector."

"We are grateful that you found the murderer, Professor."

"Thank you. I do not want to miss the call for my flight."

"Please see me when you come back to Miseria."

"If you come to London in the next year, please contact me at the World Economics Association."

They shook hands. Ben returned by the same door to the security cubicle. There he found a sorry old man, stripped to his underwear as the officials gleefully pulled foreign money from his clothing.

Ben guessed that man had enough money to make a deal with them, so he continued past them into the waiting room.

He felt thirsty, so he looked for the airport café. On the way he found Santiago's son, whom he had not seen since the flight to Miseria, sitting behind a counter in the tourist shop. "Hello, I never expected you here."

"Dr. Mchunguzi, are you leaving?"

"Yes. I take the night flight to London. How are you? I didn't know that you owned this store too."

"I do now," said the son abjectly.

"Are you renovating the store in the commercial district?"

Fire came into the son's eyes. "Rosa Lugner ran us out of the commercial district." He looked at Ben. "She said she wanted to build an electronics factory. We could take this tourist shop in exchange for the other property. Or she would run us out of business and we would be left with nothing!"

"How could she do that?"

"The new Minister of Foreign Trade is her nephew. She took over Traficant's store without any protest."

Ben realized that Rosa's solicitousness for his family resulted from a new reconciliation with her own. He had wondered why she seemed relieved he was departing so soon. "Didn't Traficant murder Professor Hudunu?"

"Yes. Hudunu went to see him one evening and Traficant knifed him and took him out the back gate and dumped him on the beach."

"How do you know?"

"His house servant cleaned the blood off the floor and off of Traficant's shoes. His house servant is a relative of ours."

"Where is Traficant now?"

"In Taiwan. Rosa made him her partner there in the electronics firm."

"How do you know that?"

"He sends telegrams about the business."

"So the government knows where he is?"

"Miseria does not have an extradition treaty with Taiwan, so it cannot demand his arrest and deportation to stand trial."

"It could block his business!"

"The government cannot. Rosa is the aunt of the Minister of Foreign Commerce."

"Why didn't you tell the police about the murder?"

"I was afraid of trouble."

"So now Rosa has taken everything."

"Yes."

"I am sorry." Rosa had taken advantage of Traficant and Santiago, Jr., to launch an industrial empire. Ben wondered at the power of the Trickster.

Discussion Questions

CB

Chapter 1
Big Ones and Little Ones

1. Names are very important in Africa. At a child's naming ceremony the child is introduced to relatives and receives names from them. Many have special meanings attached.

Does your first name or family name have a special meaning? Are you named after a family member or friend? Do you have a biblical name? Does your family name indicate place of origin, profession, or paternity?

Can you think of names in the Bible that have special meaning? (As you read along, keep track of names. They help tell the story.)

2. Who are "the big ones" and "the little ones" in Miseria? What educational, economic, and political advantages do "big ones" possess? How does Ben relate to big and little ones?

In the world today there are widening economic gaps between rich and poor and between continents as the following charts show. What should be said about this situation from a Christian perspective?

	Income	Trade	Bank Loans	Domestic Investment	Foreign Investment
1960–70					
Richest Fifth	70%	81%	72%	70%	73%
Poorest Fifth	2%	1%	0.3%	3.5%	3.4%
1989					
Richest Fifth	83%	81%	95%	81%	58%
Poorest Fifth	1%	1%	0.2%	1.3%	2.7%

	Population 1960 1989	Income 1960 1989	Income Growth 1965–80	Trade 1970 1989	Aid 1960 1989
Sub-Saharan Africa	7% 9%	2% 1%	0.3%	4% 1%	8% 38%
South Asia	20% 23%	3% 3%	1.8%	1% 1%	36% 18%
Southeast & East Asia except China	9% 10%	2% 3%	3.7%	4% 8%	15% 14%
China	22% 22%	3% 2%	5.7%	1% 2%	0% 6%
Arab States	4% 5%	1% 2%	2.1%	3% 4%	33% 13%
Latin America & Caribbean	7% 8%	5% 4%	1.9%	6% 3%	8% 12%
Industrial countries	31% 23%	84% 84%	2.4%	81% 81%	0% 0%

Source: United Nations Development Programme,
World Development Report 1992, Tables 3.4, 3.7.

3. In *African Religions and Philosophy,* Dr. John Mbiti points out how religion is not just a personal choice but an identification with one's communal identity:

In traditional society there are no irreligious people. To be human is to belong to the whole community, and to do so involves participating in the beliefs, ceremonies, rituals and festivals of that community. A person cannot detach himself from the religion of his group, to do so is to be severed from his roots, his foundation, his context of security, his kinships and the entire group of those who make him aware of his existence. To be without one of these corporate elements of life is to be out of the whole picture. Therefore, to be without religion amounts to self-excommunication from the entire life of society, and African peoples do not know how to exist without religion. (p. 2)

This identification with the community provides a great deal of personal security. For an African, the decision to convert to Christianity is not simply a matter of individual faith but a choice to belong to a new community.

What is your opinion of the explanation by Dean Gomez that Christian ancestors represent "a communion of saints"? Is this a Christian or a pagan belief? What does the libation ceremony represent?

How did Presbyterian faith affect Adam Smith's theories about economics? Does one have to have faith to be a good scientist?

In a society with communal identity, how do changes in jobs that accompany economic development affect religion? Do your jobs relate to your faith?

Chapter 2
Accept the Rhythm of the Drum

1. How do rituals of table seating, serving drinks, and dancing reflect the organization of traditional African society? How do they reflect the organization of modern society? How does history demonstrate who has power in society? How do academic theories reflect power in society? Do we have the same methods in American society for demonstrating status?

2. How much freedom do Miserian women have in family, professions, and social life? In what ways are African women better off selling in the traditional market rather than working in an office or home? Notice women's roles in subsequent chapters.

3. What problems does the student have in criticizing the clan elder? How would this affect him if he tried to become an entrepreneur in his own business?

4. What does the rhythm of the drum do to Ben?

Chapter 3
Near the Seat of Power

1. Where is power located in the modern world?

The following simulation exercise shows the relative economic power of African countries.

Each participant chooses a country or a bank and locates its information on the data sheet. The country should identify how much foreign capital it requires and then negotiate with banks to borrow money. The population times the growth rate is the new population each year. The new population times the per capita GNP is the new income needed to maintain the standard of living. The amount of new income needed multiplied by three is the amount of foreign capital needed to generate that new income. In addition, the country must finance its imports less its exports (that is, its annual trade deficit) and acquire capital to raise the standard of living. This simulation shows how difficult these negotiations are for African countries.

Bankers will interview country representatives individually. Foreign lending depends on riskiness of loan. Banks investigate each country's debt level, ability to pay, and political reliability and spread their loans to many countries to reduce risk.

First New York Bank	$10,000 million
Nippon Bank	$10,000 million
London River Bank	$10,000 million

Allow twenty minutes to negotiate loans, then discuss the results.

- How does it feel to be in the position of banker or African country?

- How is per capita GNP related to life expectancy?

Country	Population (in millions)	Population growth (annual %)	Per capita GNP (in US$)	Foreign capital needed annually (in US$millions)	Debt (in US$ millions)	Annual trade surplus (deficit)	Life expectancy (in years)	Defense spending as a percentage of total spending
Mozambique	16	3	110	158	4718	(605)	47	?
Ethiopia	51	3	120	551	3250	(780)	48	20
Chad	6	3	190	103	492	(250)	47	25
Malawi	8	4	200	192	1544	(164)	46	5
Zaire	37	3	220	733	10115	111	52	7
Uganda	16	3	220	317	2726	(307)	47	26
Madagascar	12	3	230	248	3400	(320)	51	5
Mali	8	3	270	194	2433	(313)	48	8
Nigeria*	116	3	290	3028	36068	7003	52	8
Niger	8	3	310	223	1829	(201)	45	6
Burkina Faso	9	3	330	267	834	(124)	48	?
Kenya	24	4	370	1065	6840	(1071)	59	?
Sudan	25	3	330	742	15383	(200)	50	8
Ghana	15	3	390	526	3498	(460)	49	24
Zambia	8	4	420	403	7223	(313)	50	3
Zimbabwe	10	3	640	576	3199	(738)	61	8
Senegal	7	3	710	447	3745	(838)	47	17
Ivory Coast	12	4	750	1080	17956	502	55	?
Morocco	25	2.4	950	1710	22097	160	62	?
Egypt	52	2.3	1001	3588	23524	(7745)	60	12
Tunisia	8	2	1440	691	7534	(1987)	67	13
Botswana	1	2	2040	122	518	458	67	6
Algeria*	25	3	2060	4635	24316	4800	65	12
South Africa	36	2	2530	5465	5000	3400	62	25
Libya*	4	3.5	5500	2310	?	10000	62	?
for comparison								
U.S.A.	250	0.8	21790	87160	162000	(234170)	76	23

*indicates major oil producer

1990 statistics from World Bank *World Development Report 1992.*

- What is the influence of population growth on need for capital?

- How much scarce capital is absorbed by military expenditures?

- Is foreign capital sufficient for African requirements?

2. What is the relationship of GNP/population to life expectancy?

What is the relationship of defense spending and prosperity?

Which African countries are able to supply their own capital?

Which African countries are dependent on foreign loans to operate?

3. What advantages and difficulties are there in the relationship of private business and government in Miseria? What role does humor play in Miserian politics?

Chapter 4
Life in the Boiler Room

1. What are conditions like for industrial and hotel workers in Miseria?

How is international air travel over sovereign nations organized?

What differences exist between the American and the Napoleonic legal systems? How do they affect business or individual rights?

What international treaties govern the dumping of toxic wastes?

2. Simulate a village meeting to discuss an agricultural development project. Each person is assigned a role secretly and plays it during the discussion. If more people are available, add more farmers and peasants, who can be men or women.

Village Chief. You open and close the meeting and recognize speakers. You want to maintain harmony in the village and good relationships between government and village elders. Some radicals have been known to try to create trouble so you must control them.

The Miseria Valley Authority. This organization is being formed to promote the development of Miseria. It has hired foreign experts and U.S.-trained nationals to draw up its plans for pipe-borne water to villages. The more villages that agree to a plan, the better the head office will view you.

You should present the two options, both of which require the village to volunteer labor to dig the trenches, to designate a person to maintain the pipes, and to contribute money: (1) $400. A small pipe connected to a spigot for drinking and washing dishes outside each cluster of houses. Rich families can extend the pipes to their kitchens. (2) $1,000. A large pipe for household and irrigation water. It will irrigate fields on what used to be pasture land.

Agricultural Engineer. You are working for a foreign aid agency and have consultancy contracts with large fertilizer and pesticide companies. You favor intensive cultivation of cash crops on irrigated land. Your agency will finance loans if the farmers agree to market all their produce to it.

Agricultural Official. The Ministry of Agriculture wants to maintain the agrarian way of life. You would like to enroll peasants in cooperatives where they get seeds and agricultural chemicals from the government. That way they can be organized to vote for the ruling party.

Farmer. You have twenty acres. Your three children attend school. They and farm laborers help you. Though you have put savings into a small store, you could liquidate your stock if the right agricultural deal comes along.

Peasant. You have four acres, a wife, four sons, and three daughters. They help you on your land and look after cattle in the village pasture. Sometimes you hire out the children to earn wages.

Your brother lost his land when he borrowed money from a merchant and could not repay. He is now a miserable agricultural laborer. You are primarily concerned that lack of rain will ruin your crops, forcing you to borrow too.

Leader of Village Women's League. Option 1 provides clean water to improve family health so that women do not have to walk one kilometer to the spring for three months during the dry season. Option 2 obliges women to increase weeding the men's fields without assurance that the men will divide the harvest or pay wages for the work.

Miseria Student Association. This association has been formed by students in colleges and high schools. Most of you grew up in the city but you have relatives in the poverty-stricken towns. You have high hopes as college-educated careerists but fear unemployment if the economy does not modernize quickly.

Miseria Secret Police. Your assignment is to blend in with student and tenant farmer groups. You should evaluate their plans in terms of potential to subvert the government. You should identify radical leaders for imprisonment if necessary. You may make proposals designed to expose the radical nature of the meeting, since your career in the secret police will be improved by successfully prosecuting radicals.

Chapter 5
The Trickster

1. Who is the Trickster in African tradition? How does he help the hero? African Christians often compare him to Satan in the book of Job. How is he similar or different? In an encyclopedia look up "Voodoo" and "Santeria," both of which represent transformations of African beliefs into

Caribbean and Latin American cultures. Vodumanyon is a Christian family name meaning "Vodu is not good."

In what form does the Trickster reappear in African-American folk tales?

2. How is knowledge of languages related to power in Miseria? How can churches cope with multiple languages?

What is the purpose of generosity in Miserian society? How does generosity demonstrate who has power in society or the church?

How does Sodu represent the economy of Miseria?

How is the medicine seller a mixture of traditional medicine and modern marketing technique?

Chapter 6
The Power of the Trickster

1. How are each of the government Ministers affected by the points made in Ben's closing speech? How would those points affect the interests of developed Western nations?

2. The United Nations is optimistic about the growth of the future world economy, as the following chart indicates. Do you agree with its predictions? Does the projected scenario offer goods news to the poor?

	Income per Person 1990	2000	Projected Increase
Developed Market Economies	$12,500	16,130	29%
Underdeveloped Economies			
high income	$980	1,200	22%
middle income	$3,270	3,770	15%
low income	$1,340	1,720	28%
	$390	490	26%
least developed	$240	270	12%
Underdeveloped exporters			
raw materials	$620	670	8%
petroleum	$1,540	1,930	26%
major manufacturers	$900	1,200	33%

Source: United Nations Department of International Economic and Social Affairs, *Overall Socio-economic Perspective of the World Economy to the Year 2000*, p. 47.